Praise for *Misfits*

"*Misfits* is funny, charming, and rebellious...just like Devin. I can't wait to see what happens next!"
        —James Riley, *New York Times* bestselling author of the
                Story Thieves series and the Revenge of Magic series

"Calonita, author of the Fairy Tale Reform School series, twists familiar stories around once again in this series starter, which places a plucky heroine in the ever-popular boarding school setting. A cliff-hanger ending will leave readers eagerly awaiting the next installment."
                                        —*Booklist*

Praise for Jen Calonita's Fairy Tale Reform School Series

"This fast-paced mash-up of fairy tales successfully tackles real-life issues such as prejudice, gender-role conformity, and self-esteem... More adventures are to come for Gilly."
                        —*Kirkus Reviews* on *Switched*

"Mermaids, fairies, trolls, and princesses abound in this creative mash-up of the Grimms' most famous characters. This whimsical tale is a surprising mixture of fable, fantasy, and true coming-of-age novel."

—*Kirkus Reviews* on *Tricked*

"An entertaining and often humorous fantasy flight. Recommended for fans of Soman Chainani, Shannon Hale, and Shannon Messenger."

—*School Library Journal*

"Gillian remains an appealing, vibrant character, whose first-person narrative with humorous, dramatic, and self-reflective touches makes for a fast-paced, entertaining read."

—*Booklist* on *Charmed*

"Fans of Calonita's previous book in the series will enjoy this continuation of the story. Tweens who are fans of fractured fairy tales like the Whatever After series by Sarah Mlynowski will have no problem getting into this read."

—*School Library Journal* on *Charmed*

"Another winner from Jen Calonita. Charming fairy-tale fun."

—Sarah Mlynowski, author of the *New York Times* bestselling Whatever After series on *Flunked*

Also by Jen Calonita

Royal Academy Rebels
Misfits
Outlaws

Fairy Tale Reform School
Flunked
Charmed
Tricked
Switched
Wished

ROYAL ACADEMY
REBELS

OUTLAWS

JEN CALONITA

sourcebooks
young readers

Published by Sourcebooks Young Readers, an imprint of Sourcebooks Kids
P.O. Box 4410, Naperville, Illinois 60567-4410
(630) 961-3900
sourcebooks.com

Library of Congress Cataloging-in-Publication Data

Names: Calonita, Jen, author.
Title: Outlaws / Jen Calonita.
Description: Naperville, IL : Sourcebooks Young Readers, [2019] | Series: Royal
    Academy rebels ; [2] | Summary: Banished to the Hollow Woods, Devin and
    her friends, old and new, devise a plan to expose the truth about evil
    fairy godmother Olivina to all of Enchantasia.
Identifiers: LCCN 2019008890 | (hardcover : alk. paper)
Subjects: | CYAC: Fairy tales--Fiction. | Characters in literature--Fiction.
    | Princesses--Fiction. | Fairy godmothers--Fiction. | Schools--Fiction. |
    Human-animal relationships--Fiction.
Classification: LCC PZ7.C1364 Out 2019 | DDC [Fic]--dc23
LC record available at https://lccn.loc.gov/2019008890

Source of Production: The Maple Press Company, York, Pennsylvania, United States
Date of Production: August 2019
Run Number: 5015806

Printed and bound in the United States of America.
MA 10 9 8 7 6 5 4 3 2 1

For my fellow outlaw Kieran Viola, a good friend with a steady arm and perfect aim

And for Brady Viola, the best first reader an author could ask for

ROYAL ACADEMY

From the Desk of the Fairy Godmother

[URGENT!]

My Dear Students:

Sweet dreams should never be interrupted with sour news, but unfortunately, that is what I must deliver this morning. I regret to inform you all that several first-year students were expelled from Royal Academy overnight.

I know this information is hard to process. Many of us (myself included!) are still recovering from last night's attack on our anniversary ball. Thankfully, we have swiftly dealt with the security breach, and our school gates will be closed to nonroyals until further notice. The safety of you—my future leaders—is our top priority!

As for the first-years who were suspended, I know many of you will have questions, which is why I wanted to reach out before any vicious rumors started.

Students are only suspended from Royal Academy in the rarest of circumstances and only after committing three offenses at school. In the history of this distinguished academy, suspensions have only occurred a handful of times and only as a last resort. Unfortunately, try as I might, I could not get through to these wayward royals. It was decided their radical ideals were too dangerous to allow them to stay among our ranks.

For your reference, these students are:

Sasha Briarwood

Logan Nederlander

Devinaria Nile

Heathcliff White

Raina White

I know the pedigree of some of these individuals is alarming—several of these students are siblings of members of the royal court—but the court backs this decision. It is heartbreaking to hear of royals who do not heed the call of duty, but ivy left untamed can overtake an entire castle. These students were attempting to change the way the world views royals and how we rule. In these uncertain times, why mess with a system that works beautifully? These students threatened this kingdom's very future with their lies.

Considering their offenses, there is to be *no* contact with the suspended individuals. If they attempt to contact you, your roommates, friends, or staff, or are seen anywhere near school grounds, call for me immediately. Failure to do so will result in *your* dismissal.

But don't despair! Follow the Royal Academy rules, remember your manners, and all your fairy-tale dreams are still sure to come true.

Forever yours in wishes,
Headmistress Olivina

◇◇◇◇◇◇◇◇

(For questions not answered here, please do not bother the headmistress. She is extremely busy! Contact her assistant, Hazel Crooksen, with any additional concerns. But truthfully, the headmistress answered all your questions already.)

THIS IS NO TIME TO PANIC

I used to daydream about spending my life wandering through the woods, helping animals in need, completely free of the responsibilities that come with being twelfth in line to the throne of Enchantasia. So you'd think being banished to a forest would be a dream come true. Expansive woodlands? Check. A plethora of wild creatures at my fingertips, just ready and waiting to be taken care of? Check. Stripped of my royal status? Check.

But if I've learned anything from my recent run-ins with a certain fairy godmother, it's "Be careful what you wish for."

Because as much as this situation seems like a dream come true, it's actually a nightmare. You see, a few hours ago, I kind of got me and my friends kicked out of Royal Academy and banished forever.

Banished as in we can't go home or see our families again.

Banished as in the whole of Enchantasia thinks we're criminal outlaws.

Headmistress Olivina dropped us in the middle of a spooky forest where the air is thick with dew and the trees cast such deep shadows I can't tell if it's night or day. The ground is wet from a recent rain, and we're surrounded by the sounds of a lonely wolf howling in the distance (it's crying about being lost from its pack, poor thing), an occasional low rumble of thunder, and sniffling.

My roommate, Raina, Snow White's younger sister, is not handling the banishment well. She is curled in a ball on a mound of leaves, holding her white gloves and crying. Her brother, Heath, is… Where is Heath? I don't see him anywhere. I can see our friend Logan picking edible berries for a possible breakfast. Logan may not be the outdoorsy type, but he knows how to whip up a meal even in the direst of circumstances. My other roommate, Sasha, Sleeping Beauty's little sister, is fiddling with the mini magical scroll she uses to run her blog to try to figure out our location.

Me? I feel dazed, confused, and quite frankly, angry. But I guess that's to be expected when your school's headmistress waves her wand and *poof*! Banishes you for not going along with her plans. Now the most beloved fairy godmother in Enchantasia is probably telling the kingdom we're a bunch of traitors when it's she who is the double-crossing, power-hungry villain.

"Drooping dragons, this is quite the mess we're in, Lily," I comment to my bearded dragon. That may sound odd, but she can understand me, just like I can understand her when she flicks her tongue at me in agreement. Communicating with animals is my gift.

Hey, that gift might be able to help us right now!

"Lily?" I call again to my lizard, who is camouflaging herself into the color of the tree trunk she's climbing. "Could you find a grasshopper or carpenter ant and ask if they know where we could find Little Red Riding Hood?"

"What?" Raina's response echoes through the early-morning air. She hobbles over to me wearing one shoe and carrying the other, which is missing a heel. Her dark-brown hair has several leaves in it, and her bow is sagging so much I'm sure it's going to fall off her head at any moment. I don't dare tell her that. One's appearance is of the utmost importance to Raina (Princess Rule 2), even if she is banished.

"Are you seriously asking your *bearded dragon* to help us find Little Red Riding Hood?"

She is pretty worked up, so I'm almost too afraid to reply. I nod slightly to Lily, who hurries up the tree trunk and out of sight to talk to some locals. "Maybe?"

"That's how you're going to fix this...*situation* we're in?" Raina can't even get herself to say the word *banished*. Her eyes are wild. "By searching for a known outlaw to help us?"

"Red isn't an outlaw," I say, sputtering.

"She's as good as an outlaw!" Raina insists. "She was in the same RA class as my sister until she left! We are not talking to an outlaw, and we are not taking directions from a dragon!"

"*Bearded* dragon." Logan looks up from the berries he's collecting. "There's a difference. Lily is a lizard, so she's not a threat like a regular dragon. Devin trusts her instincts, which means so do I. If we need to wait for Lily to find help, we will."

I smile gratefully at him while Raina glares at the two of us. Behind us, I can hear Sasha still angrily tapping at her magical scroll ("Why won't you work?" she mumbles.

"Don't we have magic out here in the woods? What's with the bad reception?")

"I don't seem to be allergic to Lily either, which is an improvement, but..." Logan sniffs the air, and his nose wrinkles slightly. "I do feel a bit stuffy and light-headed." He touches his head and sits down on a nearby rock. "Maybe a real dragon is nearby. Lily?" he yells into the mist and low-lying fog. "Find Little Red Riding Hood fast! She's our only hope at getting out of these woods alive!" He claps a hand over his mouth. "Great. Now the dragon's heard us too. Why didn't I pay more attention in my seminar, A Prince's Guide to Surviving the Forest? Why?"

"It's *Red*. Not Little Red Riding Hood, and stop yelling!" Sasha drops her scroll on the ground in disgust.

She's woven her long blond hair into a makeshift bun with the use of a stick. Leave it to Sasha to pull herself together even in the most feared forest of Enchantasia.

"She hasn't been called 'Little' since the wolf tried to eat her," Sasha adds. "Doesn't anyone besides me read *Happily Ever After Scrolls*? She runs ads for Red's Ready-for-Anything Shoppe almost weekly. She's not an outlaw," she chastises Raina. "She just didn't want to rule her village! I even heard she's starting a store franchise. Sasha looks at me and Logan. That means she isn't hanging out in a forest helping kids who've been banished for finding out their headmistress is a villain!"

Raina gets in her personal space. "Don't say such things! We don't know for certain Headmistress Olivina is evil, do we?"

Dear Raina. Always thinking the best of people, as a princess should. Logan and I are a bit more disenchanted at this point.

"We kind of do," I hear Logan say under his breath.

"Raina," Sasha says exasperatedly, hiking up the hem of her maroon dress. "Yes, we do know she's evil! Olivina knew we were on to her brainwashing ways, and she had us taken care of—and it's kind of your fault."

Raina's mouth forms a big, round O. "*My* fault?"

"Yes, your fault! You had to go and tattle on us for trying to figure out what she was up to!" Sasha's voice is rising in pitch. Logan is right. We definitely could wake a sleeping dragon.

"I was trying to save you all! You made a huge mess of things!" Raina shouts.

This could go on for a while.

"Girls! Calm down," Logan tries. "The truth is, it was both of your faults."

Oh, Logan. He's terrible at talking to princesses.

"I'm sorry?" Raina asks, but she doesn't *look* sorry.

"I was all excited to taste the roast duck with fig sauce I had suggested Chef make when, *poof*! Suddenly we're in Olivina's office learning she's the puppet master behind every fairy-tale story this kingdom has ever had—and she gets mad and sends us here." Logan rubs his stomach. "And now I'm hungry." He looks at his pile of berries. "I wonder what kind of tart I could make with these. I wonder if I could start a fire and find a small pheasant to cook…"

"Fire?" I narrow my eyes at him. "I am not breaking up an animal family by roasting one of their members for dinner!"

Logan nods. "You're a vegetarian. I respect that. I might be able to make us a salad or a soup, then."

"How can you think about food at a time like this?" Raina moans.

"Yeah! I've got so many more important thoughts rattling around in my head." Sasha starts to pace and almost trips over a boulder. "How has Olivina gotten away with brainwashing students for so long? What is she telling everyone at school about us? And how do we reach our families to tell them we're okay?"

"Hey!"

A handsome boy, a head taller than the rest of us, bursts through the trees. He's wearing a double-breasted ivory jacket with gold buttons, black pants, and shiny boots that are covered in mud.

"Where were you?" Raina sounds very unprincessy, but I guess that's allowed since Heath is her twin.

"Exploring!" Heath's blue peepers have been known to make girls pass out in the school hallways. "I walked about half a mile and climbed up a small hill that overlooked a stream. There are some caves nearby that would make a great camp till we get out of here. I doubt there are any banshees or giants in them this time of the year because it's too hot." He slaps a bothersome fly with a quick swat. In the distance, we hear a crack of thunder.

"Hmm. Might be a storm brewing. Or it could be typhira? Who can say for sure? We should start hiking to shelter," Heath says.

"Did you say...typhira?" Logan stutters before sneezing loudly. "I thought they were a myth! I definitely wouldn't want to run into one for real. They breathe fire and cause lightning storms!"

"I could swear I saw one once when I was scaling Mount Olivando." Heath shrugs. "I would have fought it off if I had to, but luckily it didn't bother us, so Father and I kept climbing."

Heath loves to mark off the places he's traveled on the fairy-tale map he had in his dorm room. His goal is to visit every kingdom in the land. He doesn't sit still, which is why Royal Academy wasn't the best fit for him either. For any of us, really. (Except Raina, who lived for the place, so I do feel badly about her being stuck out here.)

"As I said, could be a storm." Heath looks up at the tree-tops. The canopy is so thick we can't even see the sky. "Either way, we should find cover."

"Hide in a cave?" Raina is shouting now. "Are you crazy, Brother?" She holds up the bottom of her midnight-blue ball gown. "I spent months designing this dress with Marta Marigold. I am not ruining it hiking to a cave!" I don't mention the hem is torn and covered in black mud. "What we *are* going to do is call for Olivina! Fairy godmothers come when called, right?" She looks around, her eyes wild. "She can poof us right out of here to the castle where we will sort this whole mess out. It's just a misunderstanding! We could never truly be banished, could we? We are future leaders. We need to go home. She'll let us go home. Right? Right? *Right?*"

Sasha and I make eye contact. The woods are making Raina hysterical. She needs a sedative. I wonder if there are any medicinal berries nearby. Or chamomile leaves that would settle her stomach.

"Raina, she's not letting us go back to RA," Heath says gently. "We're on our own. We have to find our own way."

"Or we can find Red. Lily is already looking for her." Raina gives me a look, and I hold up the note Professor Pierce gave me right before we met with Olivina. Lily reminded me I had it in my dress when we were banished here. "The note Professor Pierce wrote is cryptic, but the line 'Be ready for anything' in the woods *has* to refer to Red. After all, her shop is called Red's Ready-for-Anything Shoppe. Professor Pierce wants us to find her. She's in the woods. I'm sure of it."

"Running back to Olivina is not going to get us anywhere," Sasha agrees. "She'll poof us somewhere remote next. Do you want to be sent to an arctic tundra run by the Ice Queen? Or banished under the sea with a sea witch?" Raina looks away.

"It's like the time we were in the burning princess tower at school—the only way we were going to get out of there was on our own," I tell her.

"Exactly!" Sasha agrees, applauding. Heath gives a whistle.

"This is our chance to save ourselves and every royal at that school who doesn't know how wicked the fairy godmother truly is." I stand up on a small rock, feeling empowered by my own words. It's as if I can hear the music crescendo in my head. Raina is staring at me now. I must be getting through to her.

"Red is here in these woods. Professor Pierce is trying to help us."

"Yes!" Logan agrees.

"I can feel it, just like I can feel an owl who is crying out for eye drops. Don't you see? Red must know how to help us stop Olivina! We're going to get the help we need to take her down and make our own future! Now who's with me?" I raise my right fist into the air, lose my balance, and slip off the mossy rock, landing in... Oh my. What is that smell?

"Uh, Devin, I think you fell in a pile of dung," Logan starts to giggle.

Heath joins him, and so does Sasha. Finally, Raina can't

help herself. As I pull myself out of the smelly muck, I can't help but let go and laugh at the absurdity of it all too.

Until a package falls from the sky and hits Logan in the head.

ANYWHERE BUT HERE

Logan goes down like a tree in a major storm. Lily appears suddenly and scrambles onto his chest. She flicks her tongue at his face as a book lands next to him, narrowly missing his right ear. We all run to his side.

"What just happened? Am I still in the forest? Did a typhira get me?" Logan's eyes are dazed.

"No, you got hit in the head by a package." Heath helps him sit up as Sasha unwraps the box. There is a scroll inside. "I think you'll live."

A dove flutters to the ground next to me and coos in my direction I look at Lily. "Did you find out anything?" I ask.

Lily flicks her tongue twice.

"Okay," I say, disappointed. "We'll have to keep looking.".

"Demetris!" I extend my arm so the dove can climb onto it. "How did you find us?"

Brynn Haun sent me, Demetris tweets.

"Brynn?" I am startled by the mention of my Royal Academy lady-in-waiting. Brynn may have been the second-to-last girl to be picked for a position at RA, but in my book, she's aces. She may not have a title, but she carries herself way more regally than I ever will. She's also back at Royal Academy with Olivina, which makes me nervous. What if Olivina has it in for her because of me? "Drooping dragons, is she okay?"

She's fine, miss! Demetris says. *She's getting reassigned in your absence.*

I clutch my chest. "Thank the fairies."

"I can't get used to this 'talking to animals' thing she's doing," Heath mutters.

"Snow talks to animals all the time," Raina reminds him.

Demetris continues to twitter. *She wrote you a note, miss, explaining everything. She said to make sure you got that book too.*

Demetris's breathing seems a bit labored. That was a heavy load for him to carry.

"Heath, can you fetch Demetris some fresh water?" I ask.

"And Lily? Go find Demetris a juicy worm or two. He must be exhausted from his journey."

I am, miss! But Brynn said getting you that package was of the utmost importance. I couldn't be seen so I came in the dark.

I stroke the bird's back. "Thank you, friend." I unroll the parchment and find not one, but two papers inside. One is a declaration from Headmistress Olivina. Just seeing her signature on the bottom of the page makes me feel as ill as a squirrel who ate too many nuts before the winter season. I read the scroll quickly and am not surprised to learn Olivina banned students at RA from communicating with us. We are officially outcasts. Grimly, I pass the note to Heath who shows it to the others. Raina audibly gasps as she reads it. Next, I open the note from Brynn.

Miss,

I hope Demetris finds you! When the scroll from the headmistress arrived in the ladies-in-waiting quarters, I feared the worst. I don't understand your banishment, miss! Most of the students (other than then wretched Clarissa) don't either! To help me cope, I decided to practice Princess Rule 43: "Never let the world see through your mask! A princess always looks happy and ready to face whatever challenge is at hand!" (I marked the page for you.) So instead, I went to your quarters to gather some of your important things.

Alas, I was too late. The headmistress must have sent someone in there already, because everything was gone. I regret not getting your animal care kit out in time.

She seems mighty angry, miss, and while her proclamation tells the students to steer clear of you all, I fear she won't do the same. She's been calling for things from her quarters all night, and Ms. Crooksen has been frantically running up and down the halls. She's afraid of something, miss, and I can't figure out what it is, but I know it must have to do with you. Please stay hidden until I can learn more about what's going on.

In the meantime, I got a copy of the Royal Academy Rules book for you. Just because you aren't at school doesn't mean you can't stay polished!

Stay safe!

Your lady-in-waiting,

Brynn

I hand Brynn's note to Sasha while Raina grabs the book and holds it to her chest. "The *Royal Academy Rules*! Thank the fairies we have something civilized to read out here!" I can hear her mumbling rules to herself as she walks off. (Princess Rule 15: When you can't find a polite way to say goodbye, don't say goodbye at all. Allow someone else to offer your regrets for you.)

"That should keep my sister calm for a while," Heath says. "Until she remembers she's still banished."

"Princess Rule 22!" we hear Raina recite from nearby. "'You can never pack too much for a journey. Will your final destination be balmy or breezy? Weather is unpredictable, so you should always be prepared for any type of—' *Ahhh!*"

Raina's high-pitched scream sends a swarm of bats flying out of a nearby tree, causing Logan to drop back down to the ground. The rest of us go running toward the sound of Raina's voice. I push my way past the trees Raina just disappeared into and find…nothing.

"Raina?" I swat away a few lingering bats (*What's all the ruckus?* I hear them screeching) as Sasha echoes my call. "Where are you?"

Heath shushes us. "Stop shouting. You'll give away our location."

"To whom?" Logan's voice wavers.

"Anyone!" Heath uses a large stick to swat palm branches in our path. I follow his example by grabbing a branch from the ground and doing the same. "We should stay out of sight till we figure out our next move. What if Olivina is watching us?"

Logan and I stare at the skyline worriedly.

"But how are we going to clear our names if we're stuck in a forest without any mini magical scrolls or Pegasus Post?" Sasha asks. "We'll have no chance to—*Aaah!*" She vanishes into thin air.

"Sasha!" Raina rushes forward at the same time I do and disappears as well. For the love of Grimm, what is going on? I rush toward them.

"Devin, STOP!"

Heath's eyes are wide with terror as he yanks Logan back by his shirt and yells at me. "Devin, listen to me. Walk backward—slowly—retracing your steps. Do not take another step forward."

I know Heath is trying to act all macho and in charge out here, but I know how to navigate a forest too. I step forward, mid–eye roll. "Heath, what are you—"

The ground disappears beneath my feet, and my body

free-falls. My scream gets lost somewhere in the darkness. I plummet down, down, down until *boing*! I hit something soft and bounce up, then down, then up again, like I'm on a cloud. It's so dark I can't even see my hand in front of my face. When I stop bouncing, I feel around for a wall or something to grab to begin the climb back up.

"Ouch!" someone says.

"Hey! You're banging into me!" says someone else.

"Sasha? Raina?" I feel around and yank someone's hair.

"That hurts!"

"Sorry!" My eyes finally adjust to the darkness. My two roommates are staring back at me.

"What just happened?" Sasha demands.

"I think it's a trap of some sort." I look up. The opening we fell through is so far away I can barely see it. But the ground is squishy, like I've heard it is in Cloud City, where most giants live.

"What kind of trap?" Raina says worriedly. "Do you think it's giants? Or trolls? Oh my bees, I really hope it's not a troll." She starts to sniffle again. "I lost the *Royal Academy Rules* book on the way down, and I just want to go home." I hear Sasha pat Raina's back as she gulps back tears.

"I don't know about home, but we are definitely getting out of here." I look around to see what our options are.

"Heath is still up there with Logan," Raina says brightly. "They can help us."

"Maybe we can bounce up and grab hold of something." I begin to spring up and down, hoping to grab onto a rock ledge. "Let's try to do it at the same time. One, two, three, and jump!" We start to bounce at the same time and crash into one another.

"*Oww, oww, oww!*" Raina complains. "It's not working. Plan B!"

"Hey, do you hear something?" Sasha asks.

I hear a distinct whooshing sound as if something is falling fast. I hope it's not Heath or Logan barreling down on us. "Watch out!" I brace myself against the cool, rocky wall and wait for something to hit the bouncy ground. Nothing does.

"It's a vine!" Sasha shouts. "The boys must be trying to pull us up."

"Oh good!" Raina cries. "*Heath!* I'm coming up first!" She grabs the vine and begins to pull herself up. "Oh!" She grimaces. "This is tougher than it looks, but I…can…do…it!"

"I'm right behind you." Sasha grabs the vine, climbing behind Raina. "This hole is giving me hives."

Once Sasha and Raina start ascending, I grab onto the rope, pulling myself hand over hand up toward whatever light I can see above us. I hope this vine can hold the three of us. The narrow passage feels like it goes on forever. Finally, I see the opening. Raina clambers out, then Sasha follows after her. I reach the top and pull myself out of the hole.

"Drooping dragons, that was some climb!" I dust myself off and stand up. "It's a good thing you found that…vine." My eyes lock on my friends, and for a moment, I don't understand what I'm seeing.

Heath, Logan, and my two roommates have been bound together and blindfolded.

This *is* a trap.

I attempt to run and feel something sharp poke me in my chest. I inhale sharply and look down. A human-sized mouse dressed as a pirate has a wooden cane pointed at my chest. It quickly blindfolds me and ties my hands together. "Wait!" I panic. "This is a misunderstanding."

"No misunderstanding," the mouse says. "You're trespassing in our forest, and it's time for you to leave."

WINGS OF FIRE

We are stumbling single-file through the forest, blind-folded and shackled, and to make matters worse, now Raina is mocking me. "I have a splendid idea: let's go find Red Riding Hood.'" Raina mocks me as we stumble blind-folded and shackled single file through the forest. "'She will want to help us!'"

"I didn't say that *exactly*," I argue. *Although I did assume. Why would Professor Pierce use the name of Red's shop in my note if it wasn't a clue?*

Unless it was just a coincidence.

No sense bringing that up now.

"'Let's wander around the dangerous woods looking for her!'" Raina adds, doing a terrible impression of my voice.

"Enough, Raina," Sasha says. "Devin didn't know she'd lead us into a trap and we'd be captured before we even got my mini magical scroll to work."

It kind of sounds like Sasha is mocking me too.

"I don't know why you like adventures, Heath," Logan says wearily. "This forest is the worst place ever."

My expert hearing tells me they're all in line behind me.

I roll my eyes under the bandanna. "Don't get hysterical. Once this mouse…er…pirate takes us to its ship, I'm sure we can straighten everything out. You'll see."

"Pirate?" Logan asks.

"Mouse?" Raina questions. "I didn't even see anyone! I was rudely blindfolded before I could even ask to wipe the mud off my nose."

"Whatever! The point is, we're going to be fine," I insist. I think it's important to be a glass-half-full kind of girl.

"I wouldn't be so sure about that," the pirate mouse says with a deep laugh.

We're yanked to a stop, and my blindfold is ripped off.

I blink rapidly as I stare up at a bright-blue sky. Where did the forest go? And why do I feel like I'm standing on a cloud? I look down. Oh, yes. I see now. I am standing at the edge of a cliff.

A waterfall is flowing a few feet away from us, crashing into a deep abyss below. I can't see the bottom of the ravine, but I can see the angry, rushing water. I try to take a step back and feel a poke in my back.

"Don't move!" the pirate mouse barks. He has his cane pointed at me again. It's rather pointy.

"Look, we don't want to be like Humpty Dumpty and have a great fall, okay?" Logan says. The mouse has removed the others' blindfolds as well. "Heights make me dizzy. Could we please move away from the ledge?"

"We're not here to hurt you," Heath sounds calm. "We were lost and trying to find someone who could help us."

"Red Riding Hood is not your friend," says the pirate mouse. "She doesn't even know you."

"You know Red?" I ask excitedly, straining to see my captors. There are three of them. How did he know? Maybe Lily spoke to a local who told the mice who we were looking for!

"Stop talking! We're the ones doing the talking, you see? And we want you to leave."

"No problem," says Sasha. "We don't even want to be in the woods."

"Good! We don't want you here!" says a mouse with a squeaky voice. "We want you to go home."

"We can't go home." Raina's voice waffles. "We've been banished."

"Banished?" says the captor with the squeaky voice. "Where did you say you're from?"

"We didn't." Enough with the games. I can't negotiate if I can't see my captor. I twist around to see their faces.

All three of our captors are human-sized mice. They're covered from head to toe in gray fur, and they're wearing black sunglasses and different-colored pirate bandannas. They're each holding a wooden cane as a weapon. Long gray tails hang loosely behind them. They look awfully familiar... Are these the famous Three Blind Mice? Last I heard, they'd regrown their tails the farmer had cut off and built a house out of wood chips. I've never heard of them living a life of thievery.

"Go ahead and get a good look. Just know it will be your last," says a mouse with a red bandanna.

Carefully, my friends and I turn away from the chasm and shuffle in a line closer to our mice captors.

The first one, the one with the black bandanna, pokes me in the ribs again. "I said, 'Who are you?'" Its voice is gruffer.

"There's no need to be rough," Heath tells it. "Calm down, and we'll get you a nice piece of Gouda."

The mouse throws its cane up in the air. "Just because one mouse likes cheese doesn't mean we all like cheese. How judgmental can a pretty-boy prince be? Toss them over."

"Wait!" I shout. "You're making a huge mistake."

"You're the one who made a mistake trespassing on our land," says the mouse with the red bandanna. "Tell us what you're doing in our woods, or you're going for a lovely little ride."

The third mouse, who is wearing a blue bandanna, starts to cackle. Its voice is very high-pitched. "I wouldn't call it lovely. Or little. That's quite a long drop."

"Olivina, save us," Raina cries out.

Sasha rolls her eyes and gives Raina a sharp nudge with her elbow. "Don't you get it? Olivina's the one who sent us here. She wants us *gone*! She's not coming to save us, and if she does, it'll probably be to put us in a worse situation than we're already in."

"Wait. Did you just say Olivina?" asks the blue mouse.

"Yes," Raina continues. "She's the fairy godmother in

charge of our school, but Devin accused her of being evil and go us all kicked out of Royal Academy." She gestures to me.

"Don't forget me!" Sasha interrupts and looks at the mice. "I've been secretly gathering intel on the fairy godmother and trying to find out more about the other students she's banished." She shrugs. "But Devin rubbed Olivina the wrong way from the start."

"Thanks," I say, feeling awkward as the blue mouse continues to stare at me.

"Anyway," Raina continues, "Devin is the one who started this whole revolution at RA that we all got roped into."

"We can't trust them," the red mouse says to the blue one. "This could be a trap! What if Olivina knows where we are? We need to get rid of them fast."

The red mouse starts advancing on us and Raina shrieks. If we back up any more, we'll be over the side.

"You know Olivina too, don't you?" I ask, desperate for a way to stall them. "Then you may already know what she's really like. Please. We're just trying to find a way…"

"Home," Logan supplies. "Were you banished too?"

The black mouse with the gruff voice looks down. "Yes. We—"

The blue mouse hits him in the head with its cane. "No, Corden! Say nothing. We stick to the plan."

The mouse hits himself on the head. "You just said my name! We're not supposed to do that either!"

"It was an accident!"

"An accident like that could cost us our lives!" says the blue mouse.

"*Keep them talking*," Heath whispers to me as the mice bicker. He motions with his head to his bindings. He's almost got them off!

"We've been out here a long time. Aren't you tired of hiding?" Corden asks the blue mouse.

"We've got a good life here, don't we? I don't miss the village, do you?" the soft-spoken blue mouse is saying.

"I do," says the red mouse.

Heath's bindings fall to the ground. The mice don't notice.

"Devin," Logan says through gritted teeth. "Call for help. Now."

"Call for help?" I whisper. Did he hit his head harder than I thought? Who am I going to call?

"Your forest friends!" he says softly.

Of course! Why didn't I think of that? Once I open my

mouth, the mice will know we've got something up our sleeve, but maybe Heath can hold them off. It would be helpful to have something big on our side. Like a dragon!

Nah. That's too risky, and Logan could have a reaction (since he's allergic and all). Who else could I call for? A Pegasus? Hmm…we're probably too far from the village to call one. We need something with wings though. Something that will frighten a mouse. Even a giant one. Something like…a hawk.

I suck on my lips and inhale sharply, then let out the birdcall I've been working on. I'm pretty sure it works for hawks too. "*Caw! Caw-Caw-ka-caw! Caw-ka-wa!*"

Translated it means: "Help, Wings of Fury! Save us! My friends and I are being held captive! Save us!" Although my last *wa* might have meant coconuts. But it will have to do.

Corden frowns. "What's she doing?"

"*Caw! Caw! Caw!*" I call again, eyeing the treetops for a sign of help. "Save us! Help, Wings of Fury!"

The blue mouse stares at me with interest. "You're an animal whisperer! How is that possible?" It whirls around to face Corden. "Grab them! They're trying to get a—*Waah!*" Heath, now free from his bindings, dives at the blue mouse's furry feet and sends it to the ground. Its cane goes skidding across the dirt.

Logan, also free now, comes running up behind it, grabbing the mouse's cane. "I got it! I got it! Back, you rodents!"

The remaining two mice squeak and start running.

Logan beams at me. "I had no idea I could be so menacing." He waves the cane in the air. "I should carry a cane more often. Maybe it would keep the dragons away."

Raina screams. "Logan, watch *out*!"

A massive bird bursts through the canopy of leaves overhead. Its feathers are so bright red they look like they're glowing. It's double the size of a Pegasus with a wingspan as large as an entire treetop. I stare at the tuft of yellow feathers on its otherwise red head in awe. Then I notice its gigantic green claws. They look like they could slice us in half with one swipe.

"Devin, what did you do?" Sasha cries.

Drooping dragons, I didn't call a hawk. I called a creature I've only ever read about in animal guides. I've called a firebird! The bird sees me and starts to screech. I try to understand what it's saying, but I don't understand the dialect. The next thing I know, it's whooshing down to our clearing.

"It's a firebird! Run!" Heath shouts. Raina and Sasha head

for the tree line, but the rest of us are still out in the open. Heath lets go of the mouse he has captive, and we all start to run.

"You called a...a...firebird?" Logan is huffing and puffing.

"I didn't mean to," I admit. "I thought I was calling for a hawk, but I think something got lost in translation."

Logan looks like he might hyperventilate. "They're full of omens! They bring doom! And they only appear at the start of long journeys and—*Aaah!* It's coming to get me!"

The bird is swooping down toward the two of us. I make eye contact, but I'm too stunned to speak. The bird does *not* look friendly, and I'm scared anything else I say might make it even angrier. I knock Logan out of the way and prepare to slide to the ground next to him, but I'm not quick enough. I feel a claw snag my dress, and my feet lift off the ground. I kick out, trying to get free when the firebird dives again, grabbing a fleeing Logan with its free claw.

"Noooo!" Logan shouts as we start to rise. "Where is it taking us?"

"I don't know!" I shout. The wind is rushing past my ears as each flap of the bird's wings pulls us higher.

Ping! Something pelts me in the leg, and I look down.

Heath and my roommates are throwing things at us! Fairy be. They're going to get us killed.

The firebird takes a pinecone to the wing and screeches in annoyance before diving fast with us along for the ride. Logan and I scream. I feel us whooshing toward the ground at an alarming speed and wonder if the bird even remembers we're still under here. We're about to become pancakes.

"*Caw-caw! Ca-ca-ca-ca!*" I shout, because I'm pretty sure that means "Please put us down!" But the firebird either doesn't hear us or doesn't want to, because instead, it uses our dangling legs to send the others diving to the ground. It takes off again, soaring into the sky.

For a moment, I see just how vast this forest really is. It goes on for what feels like an eternity, spreading all the way to the snowcapped mountains at the edge of Enchantasia off in the distance.

Then *whoosh*! The firebird lets us go.

Logan and I let out identical bloodcurdling screams as we begin to free-fall, then *plop!* We land with a slight bounce on a bed of hay.

"We're alive!" Logan shouts. "Yes! Yes!" He fist pumps the air in excitement. "Maybe the firebird was a good call after all. Where did it go?" He looks around. "Maybe it's gathering all of us first before taking us to Enchantasia Village. That would save us a hike."

Logan is so busy jabbering he doesn't realize what we're sitting in. We're in a mass of sticks, hay, and leaves, and all I can see beyond the ledge of the mass is blue sky. This is not good.

"Logan!" I shake him by the shoulders. "We have to get out of here before the firebird gets back. This is not a rescue. It's his nest."

Logan's smile disappears. "His nest. That would mean…" His face looks green. "We're his breakfast?" His voice squeaks.

"Let's make him go hungry." I pull myself up and peer over the edge of the nest. We're too high to jump. "We need to climb down."

Screech!

The firebird is coming back.

"Don't look down!"

Logan pulls himself up onto the ledge. He looks like he might pass out.

"I said not to look!"

"I'm feeling woozy."

"This is no time to panic! Just do what I do and step in the same places," I say soothingly. "I climb trees all the time at home. We're going to be fine."

Screech!

"As long as we move fast!" I climb over the side and hang down. My feet graze the first limb. From this height, I can see the clearing and the firebird is on the approach. "Let's go!"

Branch by branch, we start to descend. When I look through the tree branches, I see the firebird has some-thing—or someone—hanging from its claws.

"Stay down," I whisper to Logan, who is a few branches above me.

We hear a thud in the nest above followed by a scream. I close my eyes tight, wondering what could be happening, but a moment later we hear the bird take off again. Then we hear sobbing.

"Who's up there?" I shout.

"I'm stuck!" It's the soft-spoken mouse with the blue bandana. "Who is that? My leg is stuck! Help!"

I take a deep breath and look at Logan. We can't leave

that mouse behind, no matter how much we may want to. I pull myself back up to her and look over the side. The mouse is tangled in some string the firebird must have used to make the nest. The mouse looks surprised to see me. "You!" she says almost accusingly.

"Yes, me." I bristle. "We need to get you out of here."

"I know that! I can do it myself," she says, struggling to unwind the string she's stuck in. It's not working.

I look around the nest and spy some twigs. "A piece of bark might work."

"Not strong enough," the mouse says as it continues to struggle against the vines. "You need a holly bush branch or something thorny. Look harder."

How rude. I am the one saving *her*, aren't I? I run my hands along the top of the nest, feeling for a material I could cut with. I wish I had time to really examine the nest—it's beautifully woven—but that firebird was not friendly, and it could be back any second. My hand brushes against something thick—a rosebush vine! I yank it out of the nest wall and run over to the blue mouse.

"That's going to take forever," it says. "Here, let me try." It reaches for the vine.

I pull it away. "I know what I'm doing."

"*I* live in the forest. I think I know how to do this better than you do."

"*I've* grown up in the forest," I counter, starting to wonder why I climbed back up here. "I know what I'm doing too."

"Are you two almost done?" I hear Logan's faint voice come from below. "Because I'd really like to get out of here."

I rub the thorn against the vine faster. "Almost…there…" *Snap!* It breaks. We both reach to unwind the string around the mouse's leg.

Screech!

The mouse and I look at each other. The firebird is on its way back. We get the string unwound, and I rush to the side of the nest and begin to climb over. The mouse doesn't follow. I look back.

"I can do a lot of things, but I'm not big on heights," it mumbles. "Plus, I don't have my wand with me, and I get vertigo. I'm not sure I can make the climb down. Physically I can, of course, but—"

Screech!

Did that mouse say it had a wand? I don't have time to

ask why. I grab the mouse's hand and yank it to the side of the nest. "There's a first time for everything. It's climb or be firebird breakfast."

"Devin!" Logan cries. "We've got to go!"

I lift my leg over the side. "Come on." I offer my hand.

The mouse climbs over on its own. "I can do it. I don't *want* to, but I can."

For the love of Grimm. This mouse is more difficult than a three-hundred-pound troll. "Then follow me," I say, stepping down to the first branch. Then I climb lower and feel a yank. My dress skirt is caught on a vine. I yank it free, and the branch gives a snap.

"You know, ball gowns aren't the best attire for life in the forest," the mouse says wryly.

I grit my teeth. If I had my way, Marta, the Royal Academy tailor I adored, would have hidden pants in this gown too. Wouldn't the mouse have been surprised when I tore off my skirt! But no. I got caught up in the *Royal Academy Rules* and followed Rule 16. ("A princess shall only be seen wearing pants if there is absolutely, positively no other garment available.") "I'll remember that," I tell her. "Just climb."

We follow Logan's descent branch by branch through

the darkness of the leafy treetop. We're more than halfway down when I hear the firebird screech again. It's close now. Too close.

"It sounds mad. I think it knows we're gone," Logan says worriedly.

"Keep going," I say. "It's only a few more—"

CAW!

We look up and see the firebird's beak poking through the leaves, squawking angrily at us. It pecks at the tree, sending some of the branches swaying.

"I'm going to fall!" Logan cries.

"So am I!" says the mouse.

"Hold on!" I shout as a flaming arrow shoots past my face. Then another. And another. I look down.

Heath, Sasha, Raina, and the two remaining mice have a quiver of arrows and are lighting them up and sending them into the sky.

"Devin, Logan, watch out!" I hear Raina cry.

"Where does she expect us to go?" Logan ducks as another arrow shoots past us.

"Just keep going," I say, climbing faster. I pull the mouse along with me as the tree sways. I can hear the firebird cawing angrily, but I can't make out a word it's saying. (It's definitely not looking for coconuts.) I climb faster, reaching the ground before the others. Logan jumps down seconds later, but the mouse, somehow, is still above us. She's holding on tight, refusing to let go. Above her, I see the tree ignite. The firebird sees it, too, and shakes the branches harder. The mouse wobbles, then starts to fall.

"No!" the other mice shout.

My roommates and I stand side by side and hold out our gigantic ball gown skirts like they're nets. The other mice see what's happening and run over to spot us. The force of the mouse's fall hits the skirts and pulls us all to the ground, but the mouse, thankfully, is okay. I guess ball gowns are useful for something! Embers rain down from the tree branches above.

"Fire!" Corden shouts.

"This tree is going to come down!" Heath shouts. "We have to move!"

We dash out of the way as branches begin to fall. I hear a loud screech and see the firebird take off into the sky. I can hear the trunk of the tree splintering as we race into the clearing. We watch as it hits the ground so hard that it slides right off the cliff into the ravine. We're all speechless.

"Well, that was intense," Sasha says, squeezing me tight.

"That truly was scary!" I said as my friends and I embrace.

Logan walks a few paces away and bends down to pick up something off the ground.

It's a large, glowing feather. His lower lip trembles. "Good ogres, no."

"What's wrong?" Raina asks, clinging to her brother.

"When a firebird leaves behind a feather, it's bad luck," Logan tells us.

"Maybe not," a voice behind me says. We turn around and watch in wonder as Corden pulls off his fur to reveal a human underneath. Logan squeaks in surprise. "You said you're looking for Red, right?"

I nod.

"Maybe we can help."

OVER THE RIVER AND
THROUGH THE WOODS

Absolutely not! We are not helping them!" says the blue mouse. The mice are huddled together talking, but they're not exactly being quiet. We can hear everything they are saying.

"They just saved your life!" Corden argues, his face turning red. "I don't think they're here on Olivina's orders. They're lost. Just like we were."

"Yeah, come on, Tara," says the red mouse as it shrugs out of its costume and reveals a girl with red hair and a face covered in silvery glitter. "They're just like us—banished. Why can't we help them? We have the room."

"Yes, but we are not taking in strays!"

"Strays?" Logan repeats, looking at me. "I feel like a cat."

"We're sticking together. Just the three of us. That was our rule," Tara, the blue mouse, says.

"Rules change," says the girl with shimmer on her face.

Tara sighs and steps out of her costume. Raina gasps. The girl is beautiful. She has dark-amber skin, and her hair hangs in at least six braids that swing as she paces back and forth. When she turns to talk to Corden, I glimpse a sprinkle of freckles across her nose. "No. Rules keep us safe. This is my forest, and they're trouble! I can tell. We cannot take them home."

I bristle. *My* forest? Who says, "*My* forest?" As if anyone could actually *own* the forest! The forest belongs to every living creature in it, not a girl who tricked us into believing she was a mouse and tried to send us over a waterfall.

"We can't just leave them out here," says Corden. "They won't survive."

"We were doing fine on our own before you grabbed us." I look to my friends for backup.

Logan shakes his head. "Not really."

"Not even a little bit," Sasha agrees.

"I don't care. They can't stay," Tara says again. "They'll draw too much attention. She's never banished this many students at once before. We were all banished separately."

Her face darkens. "This situation has trouble written all over it."

"Plus, there is the firebird feather." Logan holds it up. "That's another bad omen."

"Whose side are you on?" Heath asks. "Look, we don't want to move in to your...camp or whatever it is you have out here."

"Yeah!" I second. Who needs this Tara and her bossy ways? We can figure this out without her.

"We're just tired. Dirty. Hungry." Heath gives his famous heart-melting smile. "If we could make camp with you for one night, we'd be on our way tomorrow." The girl with shimmer starts to giggle.

"It's one night, Tara. Let them stay," she says.

"Do you have a pop-up castle? Or maybe a luxury tent? I'd be fine with either," Raina says.

Shimmer girl opens her mouth. "It's..."

Tara clears her throat. She looks at her and Corden. "Fine. They can stay for *one* night, Prue. Then they're on their own."

"Thank you!" Raina starts walking. "I am desperate for a wash, and I'd love some moisturizer. I don't suspect you have those all the way out here, do you?"

Corden grins. "Of course I do. Skin gets too dry out here without it. I make my own, actually."

Raina loops her arm through his. "Will you share some?" Sasha, Logan, and Heath follow them.

"So where are we heading, anyway?" I grumble to Tara. "You didn't actually say."

She barely looks at me. "You'll see when we get there."

Ogre's breath, she's secretive! Now I'm dragging my heavy, dirty skirt through the mud, wishing I was wearing pants, while her and her non-mouse buddies carve a path through some heavy brush for us.

Humph! A flicker of movement on a nearby tree, and my heart flutters when I see it's Lily. I haven't seen her since the firebird attack. Smart little bearded dragon. I knew she'd find us again! I scoop her up and slip her into my skirt pocket.

Sasha appears at my side and whispers in my right ear. "It's her, isn't it?" She doesn't wait for my response. "It has to be!"

"Who is *her*?" I ask, glaring at Tara as she walks ahead of me.

"Tara! She's the princess who was banished before us," Sasha says excitedly, as if this should be obvious. "Think about it: How many Taras in the kingdom do you know?

She looks around our age—probably a year older—and she's hiding out in the forest with two friends who are equally worked up about Olivina. It's her!"

I'm too flabbergasted to respond. This girl is *the* Tara? The one who was on to Olivina before we even arrived? Naah…

Sasha's blue eyes widen. "If it's her, Tara might know something about Olivina we can use to get out of this banishment. I know what you're thinking: Why do I want to reverse the banishment? It's not like I want to go back to RA to study, unless someone else takes over who is more progressive in their teaching methods, but I don't want to be banished from the kingdom."

I point to the trees around us. "If you haven't noticed, this Tara seems happy in the woods and wants us gone. I don't think she's interested in figuring out how to reverse our banishment."

"She knows something." Sasha is pensive. "Look at her."

We both study the girl leading the way. She keeps looking around like she's worried something's going to jump out and attack us.

"Maybe."

Sasha prides herself on her sleuthing skills, so I let her run with the theory. She's got to be a good reporter to run her own fairy-tale blog—the *Enchantasia Insider*. Few people know Sleeping Beauty's younger sister runs the blog. I still feel guilty she won't be able to publish it now that she's been banished.

"Unless she's hiding out till she figures out how to take down Olivina and gathers more allies to stop her," Sasha adds. "Allies like Red! I'm telling you: This is the princess Olivina doesn't want anyone knowing about. Olivina's afraid of this girl. The question is: What does she know about the fairy godmother that we don't?"

"Did you say this air is making you bloat?" Heath whispers, appearing on my other side. "Because I agree. I never would have eaten three slices of roast pheasant last night if I knew I'd be hiking the forest before dawn this morning."

Logan holds his stomach. "Oh, roast pheasant." He shakes his head. "I miss having access to a kitchen already."

I feel my stomach tighten. Like Sasha, Logan never would have been mixed up in this mess with Olivina if it hadn't been for me. Helping me save that baby dragon egg, fighting gargoyles, disobeying the school rules—him being involved was all my fault.

"Never hike without water," Heath lectures. "This one time, we were climbing down Hobshead Canyon, and a pack of wolves showed up out of nowhere and—"

"Heath! Focus! We were talking about Tara," says Sasha. "We think she's the princess who was banished from RA before us."

Heath leans against a tree to think. The trunk has a WANTED poster for Robin Hood on it. He's legendary in these parts for stealing from the rich and giving to the poor—and he's never been found. "Tara… Should I know a Tara? She doesn't look familiar, and believe me, I know most of the young ladies in this kingdom." He winks at us, and we both roll our eyes.

"We think she had our dorm room before us," I supply. "But we could never figure out why she was banished. Snow knew her but wouldn't say what happened."

"We should find out her last name," Heath suggests. "Maybe then we can figure out what royal family she's part of."

"Good idea! We will have to find out a way to ask her. Maybe she arrived at Royal Academy a totally unknown royal." Sasha looks at me. "Kind of like you."

I try not to bristle. Tara and I are nothing alike.

Tara looks back suspiciously. "All okay back there?"

"We're fine," Heath tells her, "but if you'd like a hand with blazing that trail, I can help." He flexes his biceps.

Tara gives him a withering glance. "I'm fine on my own, thanks, but stay close." She shields her eyes and looks upward. "A storm is coming. We need to be inside before it gets here. I know the way around this forest better than anyone."

"Again with this?" I mumble.

Heath nudges me. "What's wrong with you? Aside from the fact we've been ejected from the kingdom?"

"I'm fine." *Aside from being ejected from the kingdom.* "I just don't trust her…or them." Up ahead, Raina still has her arm around Corden and the two are laughing.

"Why? They didn't abandon us. They're taking us back with them," Heath argues.

"After originally trying to make us disappear for setting foot on their property," I remind him. I watch Tara closely.

"It was a misunderstanding!" Sasha counters. "We've smoothed things over. We've got a place to stay for a day, and we can use that time to learn who they are, what they're doing out here, and why they were banished. Hopefully, they can put us in touch with Red too. It's going to be fine." She nudges Heath and me forward. "Now let's try to be more social and make nice. Trust goes both ways, you know."

"But your mice costumes looked *so* real," I hear Raina say as we approach the group. "They were brilliant! How did you make them so lifelike? I never would have known you were human. Never!"

"Thanks," Corden says as he helps Raina over a rock in her path. His nails are painted black, and he's wearing eyeliner. A skull earring dangles from his right ear, and another skull appears on his weathered black-leather vest. Underneath he has on a white shirt that looks fashionably distressed and bright-red leather pants. "I've been working on those costumes for a while now. Sewing is a hobby of mine."

"Hobby?" Tara repeats, turning to look at Raina. "Don't let him fool you. Corden is a master of disguises. How do you think Robin Hood's Merry Men get around without being seen? Last week, Corden dressed a bunch of them up as garden gnomes. Every time someone turned around, they froze. It was excellent!"

Corden shrugs. "It was all right. My best costume so far was a black bear. Friar Tuck was able to get into the Three Little Pigs restaurant without anyone bothering him." He starts to belly laugh. "You should have seen it! The pigs went running. I even gave Tuck a voice changer, which gave him a ferocious growl." Raina's pink mouth widens in an O shape.

"And the costumes disappear seconds after taking them off, so there's no evidence," Prue adds. "It's Corden's most amazing trick."

"A better trick would be getting you to let me give you a makeover." His pale-blue eyes widen. "I am dying to try some of these face elixirs and lip stains I've made on someone, but both Prue and Tara are anti-frills. I am in desperate need of a muse."

Raina grabs Corden's arm's tighter. "Search no further; I'll be your muse. The minute we get to the... Where are we going anyway?" I hear a rumble of thunder in the distance.

Tara slashes again, and the brush falls to the side, revealing a clearing. "Here we are! Home, sweet home! Let's get you inside. Quickly."

Logan blinks. "There's nothing here."

"Think again," Corden says with glee. "Prue here is a master at the protection skill." He motions to the girl with the shimmery pale skin.

"We're a clever lot," Tara boasts. "It's how we've survived in the forest this long without falling down a shaft or being thrown over the falls."

I bite my tongue.

"Watch." Corden picks up a small rock and throws it into the air. The air shimmers and, for a brief second, I see the outline of a tree where there was only grass a moment before.

"I saw something!" Raina says excitedly. "Was that a house on stilts?"

"It's a tree house," Corden explains. "It's completely invisible to the naked eye. Or the magical one."

"Magical?" Logan questions.

"Enchantasia didn't want us, so why should it get to know where we're hiding out? Tara asks. "We take every precaution to protect ourselves out here in our woods. So when your lot in your coronation ball getups and less-than-sensible shoes showed up on our radar, we thought you might be here on Olivina's orders. We had to get you off our scent."

"We wouldn't have really thrown you over the falls," Prue insists. "We were just hoping to scare you off. And then the firebird showed up."

"Oh, you scared us all right," Logan says as raindrops

begin to fall. "So did the firebird." A clap of thunder makes everyone jump.

"Enough dawdling." Tara walks to the center of the clearing and mumbles a few words while sprinkling something from a sack. A moment later, a tree house appears high in an oak tree.

It's nothing like the kind of tree house I begged Father to make me when I was younger. This one looks like a pirate ship. There are chutes and ladders connecting each level, a crow's nest, and a smokestack and large antennae at the top. The tree house is painted a green color that camouflages it against the trees, and it's so high off the ground that you'd never notice it unless you looked up.

Prue passes out small satchels. "This is Mirage Mix. It's the only way you can get up in the tree house—with the password, of course." She looks at us. "Tara's already said it, so you're good to go for the next sixty seconds till the tree house disappears again. Watch." Prue runs into the clearing, throws the dust into the air, and disappears.

"Next." Tara motions to Heath. "I'll be last up to close the protection spell again. Hurry!"

Logan looks worriedly at me as Heath jogs past him and

disappears. Corden takes Raina's hand, and the two of them disappear. One by one, everyone disappears until only Tara and I are left.

"Devin!" Logan calls down to me. "It's okay! Come up. The ride is great!"

Ride?

"You better get going, Princess," Tara tells me. "Or this opening is going to close. I'm not sure you're cut out for this storm that's brewing."

I square my shoulders as the wind picks up. "I'm sure I've seen worse." I reach down to pick up Lily and put her into my pocket, then I jog into the clearing and place some dust in my hand as the thunder booms closer. Then I close my eyes and blow the dust into the wind. My body is sucked up so fast, I don't even have time to scream. I feel myself whooshed through an invisible tunnel as if I've been catapulted into the sky, and then, *boom*! I land on a Technicolor pirate deck that smells like cinnamon and apples.

I'm taking a deep whiff when my arms are lifted by two mechanical arms. I kick out in a panic, but am quickly placed on a giant *X* that marks the spot. I'm doused with water and soap that makes me sputter (even if it tastes like licorice) and then dried just as fast. The nicks on my arms from climbing down from the firebird's nest are somehow gone too.

"Presenting Devinaria Nile of Cobblestone Creek," a tinny voice from beyond declares. "Animal lover, reluctant princess, and lover of trousers. When in residence, she'd be more comfortable wearing something like this!"

The muddy, much-too-heavy ball gown that I've been wearing since the anniversary party the night before disappears, replaced with a shorter blue dress, my favorite polka-dot leggings, and a purple robe with a hood. My footwear has been upgraded to boots. The mechanical arms disappear, and I'm free to move around in my incredibly perfect, clean, and warm outfit. Lily pokes her head out of a pocket in my new dress, looking around, bewildered.

"This pirate ship is incredible," I whisper.

Thump! "Of course, it is," Tara says, landing behind me. "I created it."

GOONS, GADGETS, AND GUESSING GAMES

W ho did you say created this ship?" Prue's glittery face
sparkles as she waits for an answer. She twirls her long
red hair up into a bun and holds it in place with a pencil.

Tara sighs. "Okay, you did. But I gave input." Prue
and Tara grin at one another. "The green camo paint was
perfection."

Prue turns and looks at me. "Forgive me for being so
rude. We still haven't been properly introduced." She holds
out her hand. "Prue Turner, former first-year at Royal
Academy. Welcome to the Tree House."

I falter for a moment and look to my friends. They've
been transformed too. Heath and Logan are clean and in
fresh clothes that look similar to their school-days look, while

Sasha is in a short pale-pink dress paired with fitted, dark-pink pants and thigh-high boots. Raina is the only one of us still wearing something formal. She's so busy admiring the quilted flowers on her new purple ball gown that she doesn't even look up.

"Devin Nile of Cobblestone Creek." I shake Prue's hand. "Nice to meet you too."

Prue winks. "I already knew you were Devin. I saw you fall from the sky last night. That's how I landed in the forest as well, but I was alone. At least you had company."

"You saw me fall?" I say in surprise.

Prue falters. "Sort of?"

"Prue is a witch," Tara says bluntly. "She sensed you all coming."

Sasha leans forward eagerly. "So Olivina banished you here too? Why?"

Tara steps between her and Prue. "Probably for the same reason she banished all of you. Everyone knows Olivina doesn't like being questioned or threatened." Tara sits down on a giant sack that says MIRAGE MIX: ALWAYS STOCK UP! "There's no point rehashing how we all got here. What's done is done."

Everyone is quiet for a moment, but Sasha can't hold

back her questions. "So how'd you upset her? Did you break into the restricted section in the library, research her origin story, and get caught?"

The thunder booms and rattles the ship, and a curtain behind Tara stirs. I'm suddenly very aware of a strange beeping sound coming from behind it. Tara's face darkens. She glances at Prue.

"I led a protest in the Royal Underground school mall over the lack of sorcery classes," Prue blurts out. "I made a big speech about how it was prejudiced to think a girl couldn't be a princess *and* a witch. Why can't a person be both?" She fills a vial with a purple slime-like substance from a bubbling cauldron.

"Agreed!" Sasha says knowingly. "My sleuthing put me on her radar."

"I was punished for helping students with their hair and wardrobe when that job is supposed to belong to people like Marta, according to Olivina," Corden tells us. "She felt I should be working in the metal workshop crafting the perfect sword instead of creating a smudge-proof twenty-four-hour lip stain."

Heath shakes his head. "I'm not even sure how I got here. I didn't love RA, but I got tossed out with only one warning."

Raina bursts into tears. "And I only had two, technically.

One was from when Devin led a whole group of princesses to illegally exit a tower exercise."

"They don't need to hear about all this," I say hastily, side-eyeing Tara. I'm not sure I want her knowing everything about us and our situation, especially since she doesn't seem too keen to offer up her own story.

"The tower exercise," Corden and Prue say knowingly.

"To be fair to Devin, the tower was on fire, and the princes couldn't get through," Raina says thoughtfully. "Devin helped us get free and climb down on our own, and then Olivina and her assistant, Hazel Crooksen, got mad…"

"Hazel!" Prue covers her face with her hands.

"I don't miss her," Corden agrees.

"I don't think everyone needs to trade war stories," Tara says, trying to interject.

"Before that, Olivina was already upset about this creature care class Devin convinced her to offer that my sister, Snow, ran," Raina continues, ignoring Tara. "It only had one session because a dragon got loose in the school—"

"Your sister is Snow White?" Prue cuts in. "And you still were kicked out?"

Heath raises his hand. "She's my sister too. We're twins."

He points to Sasha. "This one is Princess Rose's sister, and she was also banished."

"*Heath*," I say through gritted teeth.

Tara and Prue look at each other.

"If she's banishing siblings of the royal courts, she must be feeling threatened," Prue says to Tara.

"Threatened about what?" I can't help asking.

Tara narrows her eyes at me. "None of your beeswax."

"I told you we couldn't trust them," I say in exasperation. "Let's get out of here." I start marching toward a slide that I assume will lead me down from the tree house.

"Good!" Tara snaps back. "We don't want you here anyway."

The deck is quiet except for the sound of wind whistling and rain pattering against an imaginary roof. We stare each other down.

"Guys, this is silly," says Prue. "We're all in the same boat."

"Prue is right," Logan says. "It's raining, and we're tired. Can't we all just—"

A sound like a whistling teakettle begins to blare, and Tara, Prue, and Corden look at each other in panic.

Prue closes her eyes tight. "She knows they're here."

"Places!" Tara shouts, and they rush to the other end of

the deck, standing under a green chute that hangs above their heads. Vegetables rain down from above, and Prue quickly passes them out to the rest of us.

"Radishes," she says, sounding slightly concerned. "Just in case."

"Just in case of what?" Logan asks, turning as green as Prue's dress. "Who's coming?" Logan sneezes violently. "It's dragons, isn't it? I should have mentioned this before, but I'm highly allergic to all mythical creatures that might want to eat me. Particularly dragons."

"Radishes?" Heath turns the small, bright-purple vegetable around in his hands. "Who are we going to fight with vegetables?"

"Gargoyles hate radishes," I tell him as Lily pokes out of my pocket to see what the commotion is about. "The scent makes them fall asleep."

Tara jumps into the crow's nest basket and begins pulling herself up. "Don't throw those unless we tell you to. There's a radish shortage in Enchantasia—all the crops are drying up. You know what? Just stay out of our way unless we ask for your help. Which we probably won't."

I roll my eyes.

"Gargoyles?" Raina cries. "What do they want with us?"

"Usually they're out looking for us, but tonight they're searching for you," Prue says as she sits down on the edge of the deck with a pile of vegetables at the ready. "Olivina is desperate to know where we all are, but with the spells I put on this tree house, she can't find us. Which is good and bad, I guess. It drives her mad, but it also means that most days we're..."

"Trapped." Corden completes the sentence, and they look at one another.

"But we're safe, which is what's most important," Tara adds.

Raina frowns. "I don't know. I don't want to make Olivina *angrier*. I just want to go home." She steps backward, and her spiked heel gets caught on the curtain hanging behind her, pulling her to the deck. The curtain comes down along with her, revealing a large gold mirror. Moving pictures show people dancing inside it. "Ooh, what is that?"

We all gather around to look. I've only seen one set of mirrors like it in my life, and they were in Olivina's office.

Raina reaches out to touch the glass. "Is that a live look at Royal Academy?"

Prue flicks her fingers and the curtain re-covers the

mirror. "That's not important right now! Come on! You need to be ready!"

Corden runs to a plank off the opposite side of the ship.

"Line up around the deck!" Tara directs us as Prue starts to mumble incantations. As she chants, a yellow glow that looks like a barrier surrounds the ship.

"Keep quiet! They still don't know our location, and we'd like to keep it that way."

I hear the screeching before they come into view. A dozen gargoyles are flying toward us. Logan grabs my arm. I forgot how terrifying they look with their molting, battered wings and weathered green bodies. The stench is awful.

The gargoyles stop in midair, feet from the ship. Their screeching grows louder and more frantic as they hover in the air. I inhale sharply and wonder if they've found us. One floats so close I fear it can hear me breathing. Logan is shaking. I raise my arm to toss the radish. Heath appears at my side, his arm raised too. I look at Prue. She motions for us to stop.

The gargoyle lingers for a moment, swaying side to side. It lets out a terrifying screech, revealing a mouth of decaying teeth. Finally, it flies off, taking the rest of the creatures with it. Heath and I lower our hands. Logan slides down onto the pirate deck in relief. Raina plops down on a barrel next to the curtain in front of the mirror. The silence is punctuated by the sound of static, followed by a voice.

"Prue, Corden, Tara, are you there? Come in if you can hear me. Urgent!"

Prue and Corden run to a map on the wall. The map is covered with small X's as if someone is looking for treasure. Instead, Prue wipes her hand along the map, and it ripples like water, and an image appears. It's a girl in a hooded cloak. She looks vaguely familiar. Tara drops down from the crow's nest and runs over.

"We're here," Tara says.

"There are gargoyles in the area," the figure tells them. "They're headed your way."

"They were here. They didn't spot us."

"Good. That's the closest they've come yet. I picked up their signal on the readiness kit I planted near the riverbank by the set of three weeping willows. When they flew past, I was sure your cover was blown."

"We're okay, Red," Prue says. "But thanks for checking in on us."

"Red?" I pipe up, rushing to the map. "Little Red Riding Hood?" Tara tries to shove me aside as the older girl removes her red hood, revealing her bright-red hair. She's wearing her signature red cloak, the one they sell in the village in her shop, Red's Ready-for-Anything Shoppe. "It's me! Devin Nile!" I cry. "Professor Pierce sent me. He said to find you. We're in trouble. We've—"

Tara cuts me off. "We found them in the forest. They've been banished, but this time feels different. We're just holding them here till we can figure out what to do with them."

I counter. "You tried to kidnap us!"

"By disguising yourself as mice," Heath adds, coming into view. He waves to the map, and Red stares at us all curiously. "Hi, Red. Heath White here. Snow's brother. We've never met, but you were once at the royal court for a self-defense seminar, and I really admired your position on taking a year off after school to find yourself."

Tara shoves him aside. "*Technically*, we didn't kidnap them."

"They did too," I insist. "I had to save her from a firebird."

"A firebird that *you* called! I was fine," Tara says.

"Firebird?" Red raises an eyebrow. "You guys tangoed with a firebird? That's not a good sign."

"I know." Logan edges in closer to be seen. He holds up the red feather he's had in his back pocket. "I keep trying to tell everyone we're in danger."

"You *are* in danger! All of you," Red stresses. "The growing resistance to Olivina's charms is putting her on edge. More students have been banished in the last two years than ever before. Before Pierce and me, no one had been ousted, but now—"

"You went to Royal Academy?" Raina cries. "And so did Professor Pierce? But he's not royal!"

"He is. We both are. Or were. We were in Olivina's second year of classes," Red explains. "My grammy was twenty-fifth in line for the throne, but my love of adventure and self-defense put Olivina on edge. Back then, we thought she just had a really narrow idea of how a royal should act. She wasn't banishing kids yet, but she knew when she didn't have one hooked. We struck an agreement, and she let Pierce and me go. But we've always had to watch our step. Over the years, it's become clear that she's up to something more than just running Royal Academy. We've bided our time, watching her and waiting for the right moment to catch her in the act."

"Act of what?" Logan asks.

"Being villainous, of course," Red says. "She's no ordinary fairy godmother. You all must know that. She runs this kingdom. She controls the royal court. She ensures her continued influence by molding all of you to do her bidding. And when you don't…" Red shrugs. "Banishment. It's easier to get rid of a few rotten apples than ruin a whole bushel. Get rid of you guys, and her secret stays secure. But she's taken her frustrations out on too many. The number of kids that don't abide by her Royal Academy rules is growing. We deserve a kingdom free from the threat of evil where those who dissent are not banished to the Hollow Woods. The group of us cheer in agreement."

Raina pushes her way up front. "Red? I'm Raina White, Heath's sister. We met at the formerly wicked stepmother's daughters' sweet sixteen party? I appreciate your view, but the truth is, I just want to go home."

"I know you do," Red says kindly. "We want you to be able to go home too, and hopefully you will, but…" She hesitates. "Olivina shouldn't be allowed to dictate how you live your life. We can't continue to stay quiet and live in fear of her wrath. We have to fight back. That's why Pierce and I agreed you should find Tara and her friends. You need to work together."

"*You* sent them here?" Tara asks at the same time I say, "You know who I am?"

"Yes," Red says in answer to both of us as she pulls her cloak up again. "Pierce and I are doing all we can on the outside, but our names are too well-known to do much on the ground yet. It's up to you all to figure out a way to expose Olivina so we can change the public opinion about her."

"But—" Tara and I protest.

"Trust one another. Play to your strengths. You have a lot of them," Red adds.

"But..." Tara and I say again.

"It's time we take our power back, but we can only do that if we work together." Red looks behind her. "Coming!" She turns back to us. "Customers," she whispers. "I've got to go. Good luck. I'll have my associate touch base with you soon."

Associate?

The map returns to its original state. We're all quiet.

"So let me get this straight: Red Riding Hood and Professor Pierce went to Royal Academy? Who knew" Sasha shakes her head. "This would make a great blog post. I write the *Enchantasia Insider*," she says proudly.

"No way!" Corden says. "I love that scroll. We read it on the mirror Prue hacked into." He pulls the curtain off the mirror Raina found earlier. She goes running over.

"I knew it was magic!" she says.

"Don't show them all our toys!" Tara protests. She seems as unhappy with this unholy alliance Red is asking for as I am.

Prue walks to the mirror. "It's simple really. A few enchantments, an elixir for cracking the magical codes and hacking into the feed, and voilà! We can watch Olivina and Royal Academy live twenty-four hours a day. I may have sensed your arrival, but this was how we truly knew where you were going to land."

Raina walks to the mirror and caresses it. "Look! They're in the Royal Underground doing a dress fitting with Marta." Her shoulders slump. "I was supposed to have one of those today."

"You can do one here instead," Corden suggests. "I've got loads of material I'm dying to try out for costumes. I'd be happy to whip you up something."

"Really?" Raina looks pleased. "Do you think we could work up here by the mirror? I want to watch Clarissa's fitting to see if she's trying to copy my dress for the masquerade ball." Her face darkens. "I bet she tries to get Marta to give her my design now that I'm not there." She looks thoughtful. "Can this mirror see other places in the castle?"

"It can see everything," Prue says with a laugh. She punches a few buttons, stirs something into a pot below the mirror, and the screen splits into four scenes—Olivina's empty office, the dining halls, and the girls' dorm hall, in addition to the Royal Underground. Raina gasps.

"There's Hazel!" Raina points to the top left image. "I bet she's about to give out the superlatives for the week." She sighs. "I wonder if I would have won if I was there. Do you guys mind if I watch?" she says hopefully. "Please? Just for a moment? This is fascinating…"

I look angrily at Tara. "Wait a minute! If you can see everything going on at Royal Academy, then you must have seen us in Olivina's office when she banished us!"

We all look at Tara. Prue and Corden appear guilty. I'm more angry than a porcupine that has lost some spikes.

"I can't believe this! You knew we were innocent, and you came after us anyway?"

"Innocent?" Tara counters. "You're dangerous!"

"Dangerous?" I repeat, offended.

"Yes," Tara says emphatically. "We may not get to live in

the real world with everyone else, but at least we're safe here. If Olivina was mad enough to banish you all, she'll put all of her firepower into finding you. And if she finds you, she finds us. There's no way we'll be able to evade her forever." Tara sits down on a barrel in defeat. "She's much more dangerous than any of us realized," she says almost to herself as much as to us. "I didn't even get to go to Royal Academy the way the rest of you did."

"Wait, you didn't go to RA?" Sasha asks. "Because we've heard of a Tara who was at RA who had our dorm room before us. I assumed it was you."

"I never went to class. I was tutored privately," Tara explains. "Olivina said it was because she had big plans for me that no one else could know about. She kept saying I was a chosen one."

"That's what she said to me too," I whisper, and Tara and I look at one another.

"She said I was meant to help her lead Enchantasia into a new era of harmony where all villains were banished from the kingdom and we could live without fear." Tara looks at us worriedly. "But when I realized what her vision for Enchantasia meant, I ran."

"What was her vision?" Sasha presses.

"It doesn't matter." Tara's face hardens. "I wouldn't let her win, so I got out of there as quickly as I could and came to the Hollow Woods and made my own family." She smiles at Prue and Corden. "If I stay in the shadows, she can't use me to hurt anyone."

"But that's not true anymore. Olivina is hurting people now," I argue. "If she's really in league with villains, she's put the entire kingdom at danger. You hiding out here won't stop that."

Tara shakes her head. "You don't get it."

I fold my arms across my chest. "Then explain it to me."

Prue puts her arm around Tara. "Maybe Devin and Red are both right. It's time to stop hiding. We can beat her together. Then not only will the kingdom be safe, but so will you."

"Devin's right," Corden agrees. "Do that, and we can all go home."

"But this is my home," Tara says softly. "It's the only one I've ever had where I feel safe."

I love the forest too, but even I dream about a warm bed and seeing my parents again. Why wouldn't Tara want the same? I don't press it. For now, I want to focus on what Red said and work together. "You will be safe once we expose the fairy godmother for who she really is—a villain."

Raina shudders. "I hate that word—*villain*. It sounds so final, as if her story is finished and there's no hope of redemption. Why is there a Fairy Tale Reform School if people can't make themselves over?"

"There are exceptions to every rule," Prue tells her, looking at Tara. "It's time we take action."

"And how do we do that?" Tara asks, sounding exasperated. "You've been following her feed on the mirror for months and have gotten nowhere. Red has been keeping her ear to the ground for any word that someone is on to Olivina, and that hasn't happened either." She looks at us. "Your group may have gotten Olivina to admit the truth about her plans, but no one knows about it but us."

"For now," Heath agrees. "But it doesn't have to stay that way. I think I have an idea Red would like." He looks at Sasha with a devilish grin. "How badly do you want to write another blog?"

"Badly!" Sasha moans. "If I could publish one, I'd take Olivina down with my quill. I'd tell everyone what she's done. People would be shocked, and they'd have to investigate, including our own siblings. I would write the most inspiring, thought-provoking blog ever!"

"So let's get you published," Heath says.

"How? We have no way to print or distribute her stories," I remind him.

"Yeah, it's not like we can break into *Happily Ever After Scrolls* and take over their printers with Sasha's story!" Logan says with a laugh.

We all look at one another.

"Actually, I think I could arrange that," Prue says, and I can see the wheels in her head already turning.

"What are we waiting for?" I say. "Let's start planning!"

Everyone starts suggesting ideas to get into the village unseen. A loud whistle startles the group. It's Tara.

"We're not doing anything until we think this through," she says.

"Isn't that what we're doing now?" I ask.

Corden and Prue look at Tara, who smiles. "In this tree house, we take a more active approach to thinking things through. Follow me."

6

THINGS ARE LOOKING UP

*D*on't look down.

When you're fifteen feet off the ground and standing at the edge of a pirate ship plank, that's a good lesson to learn.

"I don't understand how this is supposed to help me think!" I yell to the others.

"It builds trust, and it's fun," Prue shouts from the crow's nest, high above the already-high-up tree house. She's watching the sky for any sign of trouble, but the real trouble is on the plank.

Whoever heard of jumping off a plank into thin air with no safety net?

"You're not going to fall," Prue promises. "Trust me!"

I'm not sure I trust anyone on this ship that I haven't known for more than a few hours. Then again, I don't think they trust us either. Which is how I wound up out here.

"You're more tightly wound than a Pegasus flying through a lightning storm," Tara says. She's standing on a plank a few feet away from me. "I wouldn't be out here if I thought it was dangerous."

I look down again. (Why do I never learn?) "You and I have different ideas of 'dangerous.'"

"I'll take Devin's place," Heath volunteers.

"No," Tara and I say at the same time.

"But thank you," I add.

I'm the one who agreed to think through this *Happily Ever After Scrolls* plan with Tara, but I didn't know we'd be doing it on an invisible trampoline. She started talking about an invisible trampoline Prue built off the side of the ship. "It's invisible to the naked eye, just like the rest of the tree house," she explained. Which sounded cool… until I got out onto this plank. I left Lily on the ship. I think the bouncing would make her seasick.

What if it's a trick? What if I fall fifteen feet to the ground and become flatter than a gingerbread man?

"If you want to earn my trust, this is how to do it. Just let go," Tara says. Then she steps off the deck into thin air.

Raina screams as Tara plummets to certain doom, her braids flying in the air as she falls. She looks completely calm, but I'm not. I frantically try to think of an animal that could save her from death. A Pegasus or a large bird, maybe? But that firebird incident proves my birdcalls are iffy at best.

Just as I fear Tara is about to hit the ground, she shoots straight up into the sky, past my plank with a smug smile on her face. Then she falls and bounces back up again. Just like we did in that cave yesterday.

She's telling the truth.

"See? Safe!" she yells. "Try it! It's fun!"

It's my turn. I close my eyes, take a deep breath, and step off the plank. I feel myself falling, the wind whishing past my face and hands, and then I hit what I think is the ground and bounce straight back up again. Oh. My. Goblin.

I put my legs into it, pushing down and back up again, ride. Until Tara invades my personal space.

"See?" She bounces alongside me. "Told you you'd be fine out here."

I bounce again. "Forgive me if I don't believe everything you say."

Tara bounces high above me. "The feeling is mutual."

"And yet we have to work together." I do a split in midair. I won't admit it, but this is kind of fun.

"According to Red, yes," Tara says with a sigh. "But if you think I'm going to risk all of our anonymity to help you publish a blog about Olivina, you're as crazed as the Mad Hatter."

"It's the best way to get our story heard by as many people as possible—including our families." I try falling on my back and bounce back up again.

"But the minute we leave this forest, Olivina can sense it." Tara does a somersault. "This will put all our lives at risk. Staying here and doing things from the tree house keeps us safe."

"How long have you all been stuck out here?" I ask. Tara bounces wordlessly. "If you want your situation—and ours—to change, then you have to change the way you do things. You can't keep everything the same." Tara bounces away from me. "Don't you want to find a way to stop Olivina?"

"Of course I do!" Tara snaps, scaring a few birds flying by. "But it's not as easy for me as it is for the rest of you!"

"Why is that?" I bounce over a stream beneath the invisible trampoline.

She stares at her feet as she bounces. "I told you. She said I was a chosen one. She may let the rest of you off the hook, but if she gets near me again, I'm not sure I'll ever get away. She's too powerful."

Tara's scared. I didn't see that before now. "We won't let her get you," I say, the bounce deflating out of me. "We won't leave you behind."

Tara stops bouncing too. "Promise?" she asks softly.

"I promise." Tara and I stare at each other.

"What's going on down there?" Heath calls.

The softness on Tara's face disappears. She bounces hard. "We'll do it your way, but I'm reaching out to Red again to figure out the best way to get into the village. Whatever she says goes."

"Fine." I spring up, light as air.

"It *should* be fine." Tara bristles. "I know a lot about living out here."

"I didn't say you didn't." I wonder if I could pull off a back handspring.

Tara gives me a look. "I have some tiny friends that

we've used for recon before. They could be helpful as well, but..."

"But what?" I try to back handspring and land on my face. I quickly bounce back up.

"If it doesn't work..." Tara's voice trails off.

"It's going to work," I say. "We've got a hacker witch, a pirate wardrobe genius, a killer reporter, an animal whisperer, and a couple of quick-on-their-feet royals who want to get the job done. This blog will be printed, and we'll all be free. You'll see."

"I wish that were true," Tara sounds sad, but I won't let her wallow.

"It's going to be okay," I say, like I would to any of my patients (even Chuck the groundhog, who gave me a huge scar on my arm when he bit down on me during treatment). I place my hand on her arm.

Tara shrugs it off and bounces harder, and I lose my balance. "I don't care if there's a fox in need of saving, even if you've known this particular fox since you were in diapers, Devin. We stick to the plan, and none of my friends get hurt. Got it?"

As Olivina could tell this girl, I don't like taking orders. Particularly from people as ornery as a boar with an owie.

But if my friend Fred the Fly taught me one thing, it's that you attract more flies with honey than with vinegar. "Got it. If you ask nicely," I say with faux sweetness. "Princess Rule 3: A princess—"

"Is always polite," Tara repeats and jumps high enough to pull herself onto the plank again.

I stare up at this enigma of a girl. If there's one thing I'm sure of, it's that she's not done surprising me.

Miss,   **[TOP SECRET!]**

I'm glad to hear you're safe, warm, and dry! I understand why you can't reveal your location, but I appreciate you letting me know you've found somewhere to hide till all this blows over. Hopefully, Demetris is able to find you again to deliver this letter!

Fairy Godmother Olivina does not seem to be handling your banishment well. We get daily—sometimes thrice daily—scrolls with new rules and updates on school protocol, like:

* All Pegasus Posts leaving RA are now subject to inspection before leaving the castle (which is why I sent this scroll with Demetris).
* All elective classes such as Slaying the Dragon Within, Wand What You Want, The Power of Good Wishes, and Peter the Pumpkin Eater and Other Cautionary Tales have been canceled in lieu of a refresher course in the Royal Academy rules and

daily read-aloud sessions from <u>Cursed Childhood:</u> <u>How to Avoid Being a Target for Sleeping Curses</u> <u>and Poison Apples</u>.

* Spot room checks and interviews with Hazel Crooksen are happening around the clock! This morning, poor Beatrice Sanders burst into tears when Hazel scolded her for not matching her silver heels to her jewelry. Then Patrick Monahan was sent to detention for wanding up a batch of cinnamon-sugar cookies in his room when he was supposed to be studying <u>The Prince's Guide</u> <u>to Winning a Maiden's Hand</u>. When he told Hazel he thought the book was hogwash, she nearly burst into flames!

I think your bravery in standing up to Olivina is rubbing off on other students, miss. They're starting to question the classes and Olivina being in charge of every decision about their futures. It fills me with hope!

And hope is something I need right now because I've been reassigned in your absence. I am now lady-in-waiting for Clarissa Hartwith. It's not like me to talk ill of anyone, but she is an acquired taste and a bit demanding. Her last lady-in-waiting quit Royal Academy, so there was an opening. I can see why now. I'm trying to be strong and hold tight till you return. I hope it will be soon!

Your lady-in-waiting (not Clarissa's!),

Brynn

THE PRINCE OF THIEVES

The sun is up, and today is my first—and hopefully last—time committing a crime.

It's break-in day at *Happily Ever After Scrolls*!

After enjoying a round of bouncing and a filling stew Logan made for dinner, we all tucked in for much-needed sleep.

This morning, I was woken by Demetris, my trusty dove friend, with a note from Brynn detailing the goings-on at Royal Academy. Hearing about Olivina's new rules and how she reassigned Brynn to Clarissa made me want to spit fire!

"Good morning, sleepyheads!" Prue teases. "Eat up! We have a big day ahead of us. We're finally leaving the forest!"

The ship is alive with activity. Corden is putting finishing touches on some costumes. Alongside him, a large teakettle whistles from a conveyor belt that is churning out French toast and eggs. Prue is going over plans on her magic mirror and Heath, Logan, and Sasha are already helping themselves to breakfast while Sasha tells them all she knows about *HEAS* headquarters.

"Show me the girls' dormitory!" I hear Raina say. She's standing in front of the hacked magic mirror watching a live feed of Royal Academy.

The mirror does as it's told. A grainy view of the long hallway in the girls' dorm comes into view. Brynn runs by the mirror with a neatly pressed sequin gown in her arms. "Coming through! Rush delivery for Clarissa Hartwith!" She's sweating and looks petrified.

Clarissa opens her bedroom door. "It's about time you got here! Hand me that dress."

That's no way to talk to my lady-in-waiting. Just the thought of her having to cater to that girl's every whim upsets me all over again.

I hear sobbing and look over. "That's supposed to be my dress!" Raina sputters.

Now that I really look at her, I notice the dark circles under her eyes. Has she been up watching this mirror all night?

"Marta and I worked on the design last week. I had to call in three favors to get enough crystals to bead the train of the gown. Now it's Clarissa's, and she's going to be named Miss Future Reign at the masquerade ball for sure." She slumps down. "It's the biggest event of the social calendar for first-years, other than the anniversary ball, the winter ball, and the first ball," she tells anyone within earshot.

I'm the only one paying attention.

She may be upset, but Raina has never looked more luminous. Before she started watching the mirror yesterday, Corden gave her a full beauty workup with a Genie of the Lamp skin treatment, Under the Sea kelp hair masque, new makeup, and a half-up hairstyle. Raina was so excited about the results that she stared in the mirror for over an hour. That was before Prue let it slip that Raina could watch the mirror feed of Royal Academy whenever she wanted. It's been all downhill since then.

"Ramona Mills and Charles Pullman are now in the lead for the Most Likely to Be Crowned superlative too," Raina tells me. "The new list came out last night, and I thought we might have had a shot at being on it, considering the anniversary ball was just this week, but Olivina had our names pulled. I would have won best updo, for sure."

"Raina?" Heath tries to get her attention as Corden buttons up his costume's squishy, gray arm sleeves, then magically seals them so they look natural. "You have to get dressed. Tara said Red wants us ready at 8:00 a.m. sharp."

"Ready for what?" She is still staring at the screen. "Classes don't start for another hour, unless you signed up to do the Power of Posture and Yoga seminar, which I didn't, but I can see now it would have been amazing. I was just watching Professor Hipwith unroll yoga mats in the library and—"

Heath waves a gray hand in front of her face. "Raina, we're leaving the ship. Remember? Clearing our names? Getting back our lives? Getting Olivina ousted?"

Raina cocks her head to one side. "Ousted? Olivina is the most popular headmistress Royal Academy has ever known! Hazel just announced it on the magical speaker system, and then Milo the Magic Mirror came on and told all the students how lucky they were to be taught by such a beloved fairy godmother. I don't think she's going to retire anytime soon. She's only one hundred and eighty-four and most fairy godmothers live to be at least three hundred and sixty, according to what Clarissa just looked up on her mini magical scroll so—"

Heath throws up his hands. "Prue? Can you turn that mirror off? Raina's obsessed."

"No time," Prue shouts from her crow's nest perch. She's typing away on one of five scrolls while watching another set of mirrors that show a feed of things happening in the countryside, the forest, and the village we're soon headed toward. "I need to keep all lines of magic open while I work on these access passes for *Happily Ever After Scrolls.*"

Prue found out the *Happily Ever After Scrolls* headquarters has a new intern class starting, so she added our group to today's list of visitors so we can get inside the ogre-only headquarters.

"Hey! Devin! Check out my teeth." Logan opens his mouth and displays a row of spiky pearly yellows. "Corden made me a set of false chompers. I wonder if I can eat with them. If we're going to the village, I have to stop at the Three Little Pigs. They have the most inventive fall specials."

"No eating!" Sasha slides a few bangle bracelets up her ogre arms. (Ogres love shiny things.) "We've only got till lunchtime to get this blog uploaded and added to the mini magical scroll system, or we're never going to get it printed. Prue did some digging, and according to the hate blog IHate*HappilyEverAfterScrolls*, ogres love taking long lunches so that will be our best shot at getting the blog done." She flashes us a creepy ogre grin. "I'll even sit at Misty Scorchfire's desk. I've always wanted to tell her what I really thought about her opinion piece 'Is Cerulean the New Pink?' Maybe I'll leave her a note."

"No notes!" Tara shouts from the crow's nest. She grabs hold of a pulley attached to a sandbag and lowers herself to the deck. Her oversize ogre-costume feet hit the wooden planks with a loud thud. If I didn't know any better, I'd think she was the real deal. "We leave no trace of ourselves behind." She checks her pocket watch. "Our escort should be here any moment." I hear a loud whistle. Tara smiles. "Right on time."

Someone swings onto the deck from a nearby tree. It's an older boy in peasant's clothes and muddy boots, with an quiver of arrows on his back. "Who's ready for an adventure? Hey there, Cordy!" He slaps the boy on the back, then spots me. He holds out his hand and I shake it, feeling the calluses on his palm through my costume. "Robin Hood, dear Lady Devin. It's lovely to meet you."

Sasha gasps. "*The* Robin Hood?"

He bows. "In the flesh, my lady."

Heath steps forward. "Heathcliff White." He shakes Robin's hand. "It's an honor to meet you, sir."

"Likewise, young royal rebel!" Robin says with a laugh. "Now, can we please proceed? Red said we need to move quickly, and being nimble is what I'm best at."

Robin pulls the rope toward him, and it snaps back firmly, making a tight hold. "Red was tied up today, which is why I'm here. Got a call from that Gilly girl she's been working with again. They're trying to track Rumpelstiltskin. Something about a vendetta against Fairy Tale Reform School." Robin takes in our ogre costumes. "Surprised you lot didn't wind up there after tangoing with Olivina. I, myself, was sentenced there for thieving, but I was pardoned by Professor Wolfington."

"No banishment?" Logan asks. "How come we didn't get that choice?"

He shrugs. "I was already a king so…"

"King of *thieves*," Prue reminds him. "I read all about it!

It's a self-made title. It didn't really count, and Olivina eventually realized you fudged your royal papers for admission to RA."

Robin runs a hand through his thick brown hair. "Yeah, well, it was fun while it lasted. The trouble Red and I got into for messing with Hazel Crooksen's scrolls though!" He holds his stomach and belly laughs.

"She always called you a simple trickster," Tara says wryly.

"Some might dismiss me as that." He winks at me, and I blush. Heath coughs. "Others would call me charming and roguish. Hospitable, even."

"I'm already all those things. Why aren't I leading us into blog headquarters?" Heath grumbles.

A beeping sound emanates from both a medal on Robin's chest plate and Prue's crow's nest.

"Time's a-wasting. Let's fly." Robin pulls a small red arrow out of his quiver, places it in his bow, and aims at the tree he came from only moments before. He fires and a rope shoots out behind the arrow. I listen carefully to hear it hit its target, but there is no sound. The arrow and rope seem to keep going, bobbing and weaving through the trees. A second later, I feel something brush against my head and look up. Robin is clutching the rope and flying through the forest behind the arrow.

Sasha puts her hands on her hips. "Hey! You forgot us!"

"No, he didn't." Tara grabs a quiver from a rack on the wall, shoots an arrow, and grabs onto the rope that trails behind it, looking smug as her rope pulls her out of our line of sight and into the trees.

"Well, if they can do it, so can I," says Sasha, not waiting for a lesson. She quickly aims and disappears into the forest.

"Wait, I'm not dressed yet! And neither is Raina!" I remind them.

"Dressed?" Raina turns around, confused. "Hey! Where did everyone go?" She glances back at the mirror anxiously. "We're leaving *now*? Clarissa is about to go to Professor Carrington's and learn how to write a love note. I don't want to miss it. Just give me a few more minutes."

Prue drops down from the crow's nest, adjusting the leather satchel of scrolls she's wearing over her ogre costume as she lands. "She's not ready. Maybe she should stay behind."

"We're not leaving anyone behind," I insist as Corden comes up to me and starts helping me into my ogre costume.

"Actually, someone has to stay back," Cordon tells me.

"We never leave the ship unguarded. Someone has to stay with the mirror in case Olivina makes any sudden moves. I'm staying back. She can stay with me."

"Keep an eye on her," I say as Corden seals up my ogre mask. He nods. "She'll be fine," Prue promises.

"I wish these compacts I've been working on were ready to use so you could talk to Raina back on the ship while you're in the village." Prue's eyes light up. "They look like makeup, but really they're two-way mirrors that let you talk to whoever has the other compact."

"Can we test one out?" I ask.

Prue frowns. "I don't know. Olivina doesn't like it when..." She sighs. "Sorry. Sometimes it's hard to get the fairy godmother's rules out of my head, you know?"

"I do," I agree.

"Olivina said my inventions were too daring. She said 'Princesses don't take risks, Prue!' She's wrong, but—"

"Of course she's wrong!" Corden jumps in. "You're a great witch, and your spells work. Let Devin try the compact."

She hesitates. "I can't. I'm sorry."

"It's okay." I don't want to push Prue when she's done so much already. "I'm sure Raina will be fine here with

Corden." I pause. "I should really get going, or they'll leave without me!"

"Right! Time to go!" Prue takes off, leaving me, Heath, and Logan behind. Logan stares at the quiver in his hand worriedly.

"Woo-hoo!" I hear Heath shout as he flies off behind her. "You guys have got to try this!"

"Did I ever tell you I get motion sickness?" Logan is rambling, his ogre mask drooping as he frowns. "It's true. We could never vacation far from home because long carriage rides make me ill. I had to chew on mint leaves to make it through the ride to Royal Academy without incident. I'm not sure I…"

Corden looks at me pointedly before taking an arrow from Logan's pack. I nod ever so slightly as he ties the end of the rope to Logan's pack and fires the arrow that will send Logan on his way.

Logan looks at me in horror. "Wait! I'm not ready! I'm— DEVIN!" Logan is pulled into the air and disappears.

It's my turn. I grab a quiver and do exactly what the others did before me. I pull an arrow from my pack and fire, shooting into the tree line. The rope yanks me forward without warning, whooshing me along with it. I expect to hit a tree and drop to the ground, but instead I keep going, picking up speed. Trees whiz by me, the arrow and the rope leading the way into the unknown. Lily sticks her head out of my ogre dress pocket and flicks her tongue in a way as if to ask Is this what's supposed to happen? I'm not sure.

"Lily, we have to get off this thing!" I shout. "This can't be…" *Cough! Cough!* "I think I just swallowed a fly!"

I continue to pick up speed. The arrow leads me up, down, over and around trees, mountains, even through a waterfall, though somehow I don't get wet. Suddenly we're descending, and I'm sure I'm going to crash. I close my eyes, hoping Lily is buried deep enough in my pocket that I'll be able to cushion her in the fall and—*boom!* I land hard on my feet.

I slowly unclench my eyes to see I'm standing in… Hey. Is this Enchantasia Village?

"Lady Devin, you made it!" Robin applauds. A pack of ogres surrounds him. "It's about time. We don't have all day, you know."

I try to catch my breath and look at Tara. "You…could… have…warned…me."

She shrugs. "The surprise is part of the fun."

"Too…fast…" Logan chokes out. He's hunched over a rock where it looks like he just gave up his breakfast.

Heath pats him on his back with a large ogre hand and looks at Robin. "How do you make those arrows move like that? Do you think I could get a set? I want to hike Ice Falls this winter, and they would make the trip up a breeze."

A beeping sound comes from Robin's chest plate again. He looks down and taps it. "That's my cue. I've gotten you as far as I can without being seen. Tara knows how to get you the rest of the way." Robin pulls another arrow from his quiver. "I've got a date with a king's carriage full of tax collections." He winks at us, nocks an arrow, and aims. "See you on the Wanted posters." The arrow takes flight and *whoosh*! He's gone.

THE POWER OF THE QUILL

P *sst!* Over here!" Prue calls.

Prue is huddled behind a broken-down patty-cakes cart.

I've never really understood people's obsession with patty cakes (I'm more of a hot-cross-bun kind of girl), but the cinnamon-and-brown-sugar scent that lingers around this cart *is* heavenly.

We duck behind the cart, and I'm amazed at how much Prue has done in just a few minutes. She's created her own command post. She's got several gadgets I can't identify laid out on a tarp in front of her, along with a panel of obscure buttons and pulleys that she's moving in various directions with nimble ogre fingers. Four small hand mirrors hang on a board, showing different locations: the square in front of us, the exterior of *Happily Ever After Scrolls*, the Dwarf Police Squad headquarters, and a crowded room full of ogres, heads bent over large tables, writing furiously with quills.

"That's *HEAS*'s newsroom," Prue explains as she lays a small map out in front of us. Notes are scribbled all over it. She pulls out several small scrolls and passes them around. "Your identities. Learn them. It took me all night to create each of your intern backstories."

"My name is Zol, and I'm originally from Cloud City?" Logan repeats. "Who is going to believe an ogre comes from Cloud City? I thought they liked dark places…and being on the ground."

"Yeah, like mine at least makes sense because I'm from Volcano Bay," Heath scrunches up his puffy green nose. "And my parents named me Ash, which is kind of cool."

Prue gives us a withering glance. "May I finish?"

"She spent hours researching the hiring habits of *HEAS*," Tara tells us, "and Prue is never wrong. If your ID says you come from Cloud City or Volcano Bay, there's a reason why."

"Thank you," Prue says. "Moving on." She pours a stack

of coins from a small satchel and places one in each of our grayish-green palms. "These are your identification chips. Do not lose them as they allow you access to different areas once you're inside."

Sasha claps her large ogre hands. "Finally! I've always wanted to see the printing press they use—and give that Misty Scorchfire a piece of my mind!"

"No veering from the plan." Prue points to the map with a long, brown fingernail. "Avoid the cafeteria, obviously, where most ogres will be from twelve to one, and the main conference room. There's a surprise birthday celebration there for Gangia Gordo. She's turning thirty."

"Ooh! What kind of cake?" Logan asks. "Fairy-lemon? I prefer fairy-lemon over charming chocolate."

"*Anyway*, you'll want to move quickly, avoiding areas of congestion and congregating anywhere that may cause suspicion," Prue continues. "Even as interns, you need to know where you're going. You would have toured the place before."

"How are we supposed to do that?" I ask. "No human has ever been inside. It's all ogre-run." I pick up her map with all the notes and cross-outs on it. She has poor penmanship. Who could read this? "Even if we could memorize the map, it's hard to know where we're going without having seen inside ahead of time."

Prue nods knowingly. "You're right. Which is why you're not going to be alone. I'm coming with you! Sort of."

She pulls out a small case. There are lots of holes drilled into the top. When she opens it, I see several small, gray creatures lounging on velvet pillows. They notice Prue and look up, which makes their enormous ears flap against their small bodies. They look exactly like we do as ogres, except in miniature! Several begin talking at the same time. Their voices come out like whispery squeaks. Lily pops her head out of my pocket and flicks her tongue at them. I can't tell if she's hungry or intrigued. I'm afraid to ask.

"I know! I know!" Prue is saying impatiently. She pulls something out of her pocket. It's a chocolate brownie. "I didn't forget. Sugar up. Your next assignment starts momentarily. And turn on your mirror mimickers before you forget." I notice them light up small, shiny mirrors that are dangling around their necks like jewelry. "Meet your kobolds."

"Ko-whats?" Logan repeats.

"Kobolds," Tara says with an eye roll, and I notice she's not alone with her annoyance. The little creatures are all squeaking at us. One even has his tiny hands on his tiny hips. "They're famous in these parts."

My friends and I look at one another.

"We say that because it makes them happy," Prue whispers, "but really most people know sprites better. Many kobolds live in mines and are good at getting in and out of tight spaces, obviously. They're easily offended, but great at helping with household chores, and they love the ship because they're seafaring creatures. They came aboard with Corden, and I've been training them to go on missions ever since. This will be their first real one."

"Their first?" Logan sounds even more worried. "So we're guinea pigs?"

"No, they're ready. Right, guys?" Prue asks the box, which results in more squeaking. "Trust me, you want them with you. They'll communicate with me the whole time and report back what I say. You'll know where to go based on what I see going on in the mirror. I can track you with your coins. The plan is foolproof." She motions to the box. "All right, everyone! Find someone to partner up with."

The kobolds scurry out of the box and climb up our arms. One eyes me with interest before it runs up my arm, jumps from my shoulder to my ear, and pulls itself up on my lobe. "Ow!" Instinctively, I touch my sore earlobe.

"Careful! You'll squish me!" a little voice says.

"Hey!" I tell the others. "I can understand mine."

"Of course, you can understand me." The kobold sounds annoyed. "You couldn't earlier because we were too far away. No one will hear us but you and Prue. Everyone else will just think a mouse has gotten loose somewhere, which is actually quite handy if we need a distraction. I speak more than twenty-five languages and animal dialects. How many can you speak?"

"One. Sort of. I'm good at talking to animals," I tell her. "Do you have a name?"

"Do *you*?"

"Yes. It's Devin."

"Kira," the kobold says, trying to make herself comfortable on my earlobe. She pulls some of my hair toward her to camouflage her from view. "Prue says we only have ten minutes to get to the building, so let's get moving."

Sasha is already running ahead, acting as if we're about to see the first showing at Pinocchio's Puppet Theatre. "Come on, already!" She races through the square. People dive out of the way to avoid being trampled by an ogre. "I've been waiting for this day forever!"

"That makes one of us," says Logan, following behind her. He stops short and starts to sneeze. I hear a small "bless you" squeak from his ear. "Thanks. I hope I'm not allergic to you. You aren't related to dragons in any way, are you?"

Kira talks my ear off the whole walk through the square. I'm listening, but I'm also on watch. It feels weird being out in the open, seen and yet not seen. I keep looking for any sign of Mother or Father or anyone I might know. But people are so busy their faces blur as they pass by.

"Act natural, but not too natural," Kira is saying as we approach a dead-end block called Quill Way. "Stop fidgeting. Don't pull on that heinous floral dress Corden put you in. What was he thinking? Blue and green are not a good color combination for ogres. The least he could have done was give you fun earrings. I have nothing to play with. Oh! We're here!"

I frown. This is not the village business district. Teakettle homes are percolating, a child is skipping rope on her front lawn, and a mother and her children are walking down the street, talking about what they need to buy at the market. This is definitely not where I'd expect scroll headquarters to be. "Are you sure this is the right address? I don't see a sign for *Happily Ever After Scrolls* anywhere."

Sasha pushes ahead of us. "You won't find one. The location is top secret."

"Why is that?" Heath scratches one of his ogre-sized ears.

"Do you know how many people would show up trying to get their stories published?" Sasha asks. "Or barge in yelling about a scroll post that they didn't like?" She shakes her head. "I'm sure Misty Scorchfire deals with that all the time." She touches her ear and listens to something her kobold says. "Oh! Brilliant. Okay, look for the gumball machine. We each need to chew a piece of gum to get inside."

"Gum?" Heath takes the lead. "How is that going to help us?"

"My kobold says the gum is the key." Sasha skips ahead of him. "There it is."

She rushes toward a small green square with a park bench and a sculpture between two houses. As we get closer, I realize the sculpture is actually a glass canister filled with brightly colored gumballs—it must be five feet tall. Underneath it is a sign: ONE PENCE EACH. HONOR SYSTEM! A silver bowl sits beside the canister on a stone pedestal.

"Here goes nothing." Sasha looks at us, then drops her coin into the bowl. *Zoom!* A bright-blue gumball rolls out. She pops it into her mouth and starts to chew.

"Nothing is happening," she says.

"Try blowing a bubble," Logan suggests.

Sasha gets the gum into position and blows the largest blue bubble I've ever seen. Still, nothing happens.

POP! The bubble bursts, and Sasha falls through a trapdoor in the grass. I don't even hear her scream.

"Why does everything we seem to do outside Royal Academy involve plummeting to the ground?" Logan moans.

"I could not handle this entrance every day," I agree.

Heath steps up, gets a green gumball, pops a bubble, and disappears.

One by one, we pay for our gum (mine is mint green and tastes like peppermints), and free-fall through a tube into the lobby. I land on a giant, squishy sack, then spring up before Logan can land on me seconds later.

"You're right! That was fun," Logan says to the kobold in his ear. He looks at me, grinning ear to ear. "I was nervous, but Vol said, 'Just get it over with.' So I did, and *WOW*. That wasn't bad at all!"

"Neither is this place," Tara comments. She's been exceptionally quiet up until now.

We're standing in a massive room filled with mirrors, each one showing something happening Enchantasia. There's a live feed of a royal court meeting with village officials, a fight in the mountains between dragons and the royal infantry that makes me worry about Father's whereabouts, a scene from a magic carpet race at Fairy Tale Reform School, and a live view of Royal Academy where Olivina is stepping into a giant pumpkin carriage. Some mirrors are dark, while others spring to life suddenly with ogres reporting in from around the kingdom. There is a radish shortage in the upper foothills, a fight between ogres and trolls evolving in the Snowcap Mountains, and a charity event at Jack of All Trades School. They're collecting gently used hats to sell at the Mad Hatter to raise money for someone called the Queen of Hearts.

Below the mirrors are long tables filled with ogres writing so intently that they don't even notice our arrival. Ogres walk around collecting finished scrolls and place them on a conveyor belt that moves them toward a long tube. The scrolls ride along until they get sucked up the tube and sent through a large glowing mirror near the roof. I wonder if that's the printing press.

"It is the printing press," Kira whispers in my ear. "Nice you noticed that without me telling you."

"How did you know what I was thinking?" I ask, surprised anyone other than an animal could do that.

"Kobolds are known for being intuitive," Kira says. "Besides, it's kind of obvious, isn't it? If the ogres write the stories, and the stories appear on mini magical scrolls throughout the kingdom, they have to be uploaded magically somehow. Now if only they'd shrink them down to my size so they'd be easier to read…"

A shrill bell rings, and the mirrors go dark. The conveyor belt stops, the large printing-press mirror stops glowing, and the ogres look up, seeing us for the first time.

I feel my palms begin to sweat. I glance quickly at Heath. Or is that Logan? In our ogre getups, I can't remember what anyone is wearing. Did he have on the top hat or the beret?

The ogres spring up, knocking over chairs, laughing and talking loudly. I tense up, waiting for someone to approach us, but they file past. Only one stops and stares at us strangely. "What's wrong with you lot. Aren't you coming?"

"Uh, we, uh, need to, uh…"

Logan. For sure.

"What he means is the file server needs to finish upload-ing that story about Troll Wars Boot Camp or their adver-tisement won't run in this week's scroll, and then we'll fail to fulfill our contract."

That must be Sasha.

Sasha smiles at the other ogre. "And you know how the president of Troll Wars gets when his ads don't run on time."

The other ogre blanches. "Okay, but make it quick. And only turn on one or two mirrors at most. We have to be done with lunch early to get to Gangia's birthday bash at twelve forty-five. I don't want to be late and get a small piece of cake."

Sasha salutes him. "We won't let *HEAS* down!"

The ogre shakes his head as he walks out the door. "Interns."

"How did you know about the ad?" Heath asks.

Sasha looks at him. "I didn't. But I deal with advertise-ment issues all the time, so I took a chance." She touches her ear. "Prue says we can use any empty scroll to upload our story." She pulls her parchment out of her front pocket, and I see her completed article. "I just have to rewrite it." She looks around. "Oooh, where should I sit? Would I normally sit on an end, or would I want to be smack in the middle of the action?" Her ogre eyes widen. "Maybe I can find Misty's desk!"

Kira clears her throat. "Prue says stop playing around and get going. You heard the ogre. Lunch is shorter today!"

"Right!" Sasha pulls out a velvet chair and plops down in it. "I'll be quick. You guys stand lookout."

"Prue says to activate the mirrors. You need to use your coins, but she can't seem to figure out where to put the coins in to make them work," Kira tells me. "Maybe it's another gumball machine? I had no idea ogres liked gum this much. No wonder their teeth are so rotten."

We must all be getting the same message because we quickly spread out, searching the desks for anything that looks like it could be a gumball dispenser. I notice a lot of licorice and sucking candy, but no gum. Just plenty of small signs posted on nearby walls:

WEEKEND
GETAWAY TRIP
TO

Wonderland

THOSE INTERESTED
SHOULD TALK TO CARL
BY THIS FRIDAY

IF ENCHANTASIA
TRUSTED
EVERYONE
TO PRINT THE
NEWS, ANYONE
COULD WORK HERE.
#OGRESTRONG

Save fake news for
the amateurs—
at HEAS we tell
the full story!

DON'T WORK
HARD
WORK
SMART

As Sasha writes furiously, her parchment begins to glow. When she finally reaches the end of the scroll, her words begin to sparkle and jump like they're ready to take off from the page.

"Oh, I almost forgot. Stories must be uploaded immediately, or the quill ink loses its potency. That's why ogres work so fast. They've got to get all their scrolls in before lunch or dinner," Kira adds. "Find the gumball machine yet?"

Grrr... Heath shrugs. Logan throws up his hands. Tara is on her hands and knees looking. All I see are parchment and bottles of ink. There's nothing here that looks like another gumball machine!

I feel movement in my pocket. Lily! She crawls out, shoots down my arm, and I let her run along a table. She scurries over to the nearest wall and flicks her tongue. That's when I see it. A tiny hole in the stucco. I kneel down. A pink nose and whiskers pop out of the darkness.

"What are you doing?" Kira's voice is shrill. "Tara said not to engage with anyone other than the group."

"Who's there?" says a little voice. "What do you want?"

"Hi, I'm Devin," I say. "I mean, I'm..." *What's my name again?* "I'm here with some friends. I was hoping you could help us find something."

The mouse peeks out of the hole, curious. "You heard me? How is that possible? Ogres can't talk to mice."

Okay, I'm giving myself away here.

"She's almost done!" Logan hisses.

"We need to find the coin drop to turn on the mirrors. Do you know where it is?"

The mouse looks at me curiously. Then he starts to retreat. "If you're an ogre, you should know this."

"We're, um, interns, and we're still learning," I say, but the mouse still looks skeptical. "Please! I have no time to explain, but this scroll is very important—for the whole kingdom, including mice," I plead. The mouse stares at me. "Are you hungry?" I reach into my other pocket where I know Corden packed us energy bars. I pull mine out and begin to peel off the wrapper. "If you help, I will give you this."

The mouse taps his foot impatiently. "This is a serious journalistic endeavor we're running! I don't accept bribes!" His little pink nose sniffs the air. "Although that does smell good. Is it cinnamon raisin?"

I slide it toward him. "Don't consider it a bribe. Think of it as a gift from a friend."

The mouse considers this. "Okay." It grabs a small crumb and begins to chew, talking with its little mouth full, which is hard to understand. "The gumball machine doesn't look like the one outside. When a story is done, you need to put gum in the ogre statue's mouth. It will light up the mirror and feed the scroll out to everyone who has a *Happily Ever After Scrolls* subscription."

"Thank you," I say. "Enjoy the food!" I run back to the table. "We need to find the ogre statue. It activates the mirror."

"There it is!" Tara says, pointing to a large ogre statue of *HEAS* founder, Hershel Ogreton, fashionably dressed in spectacles, a top hat, and a suit. His mouth is open wide, and the plaque below his large feet reads: ALWAYS BE READY TO LISTEN AND BE HEARD, AND ALWAYS SPEAK THE TRUTH. Below the plaque is a bowl of gum. Jackpot!

"Ready!" Sasha says and puts down the quill.

Tara grabs the gum and drops a piece in Hershel's mouth. The mirror near the roof glows as Sasha's scroll begins to bounce. Heath grabs it and drops it onto the conveyor belt. The letters glow brighter and swirl, turning the parchment bright white, then black. As the scroll is sucked up the tube, the letters disappear. Seconds later, they reappear in a mirror on the wall that has just lit up blue. The mirror begins typing the scroll line by line.

"You did it!" Kira says in awe. "I can't believe you actually did it!"

I read Sasha's writing proudly as it scrolls across the mirror.

"Okay, we're done. Let's get out of here before Gangia's party is over," Tara says.

"We need to wait till the mirror finishes writing," Heath says. "We can't risk anyone seeing what Sasha wrote."

"There's not enough time." Tara looks at the clock. "Lunch is almost over."

"We need to finish the job," I argue. "We've risked so much. We need to know this works."

Footsteps echo down the hall, and we stop arguing.

"It is here in these esteemed halls that ordinary ogre citizens do the noble work of journalism, sharing important news with the citizens of Enchantasia! That's what *Happily Ever After Scrolls* was established to do, at the urging of Fairy Godmother Olivina and the royal court. And it has done so for over three decades. Olivina and I could not be more pleased."

It's Hazel Crooksen, Olivina's faithful assistant. The tiny goblin is as terrifying as ever, strolling through the hallway in a hot-pink suit with a glittering RA crest on her jacket. Underneath, she has on a glittery ROYAL ACADEMY FIELD

Trip shirt. Behind her are ten students. All from Royal Academy.

We're toast.

She stops short when she sees us. "Oh. I thought it was ogre lunch break."

"It is." Tara speaks up, glancing quickly at the blue mirror that is still uploading Sasha's story. *If Hazel sees it...* "But when work still needs to be done, we do it. That's what interns are for."

Hazel smiles thinly. "Of course. See, children?" She motions to the RA students, some of whom look familiar. "How satisfying it is to be a regular ogre citizen of Enchantasia and do such work. This is what your lives would be like if you weren't noble. You'd live and work in this village like these peasants and have jobs at places like *Happily Ever After Scrolls.*"

Uh-oh.

Sasha stands up slowly. "Are you saying then that nobles' lives are too important to be bothered with a profession that shares the news of the kingdom?"

Hazel bristles, holding her chest. "Why, I never! An ogre talking back to a group of nobles?"

Oh no. Oh no.

Suddenly, the newsroom goes dark. Every mirror, except for the one with Sasha's story, lights up. I blanch at the familiar face in the mirror. Her white hair is piled high on her head, and she's wearing several strands of pearl necklaces.

"Hazel, is that you, darling?" Olivina says.

"Yes, Headmistress!" Hazel rushes forward, her face flush. "I've got the children on the field trip, and *this ogre*…"

Logan grabs my hand.

"Are you all right?" Olivina asks. "I felt a disturbance. Are the children safe?"

"Of course." Hazel looks confused. "Say hello to the fairy godmother, children."

"Hello, Headmistress!" they shout in unison.

"Hello, my dear royals!" Olivina's voice is thick with emotion. "I hope you are enjoying this look at quaint village life. It's nice to meet the peasants you will someday rule."

I can hear my heart thumping in my chest.

"I'll tell her who's going to rule," Sasha whispers. I stomp on her foot.

"Hello there!" Olivina suddenly notices us. "Who do we have with us on this tour?"

We all freeze.

"The interns," Hazel says breezily. "They're not very exciting, unfortunately. They're finishing some work on their lunch hour." She makes a face.

Olivina looks at us intently, her smile fading. "Work during lunch? How noble! What are your names?"

I glance up at the blue mirror. Just two more lines. My brow is perspiring.

"We're not important, Fairy Godmother," Sasha pipes up. "We're just five lowly interns."

Heath nods and starts shuffling us toward the door. "Thank you for visiting, Fairy Godmother. Enjoy your tour. We're late for Gangia's birthday party."

"Gangia?" Olivina starts to question. "Who is—?"

"Hey!" one of the students looks up. "That scroll on the mirror is written by Sasha Briarwood! Isn't she banished?"

"What?" Hazel looks from the scroll to our group.

"Sasha!" Olivina's voice goes up an octave. "How can that be?"

Kira shouts in my ear. "Get out now! While you still can!"

The blue mirror pings loud enough to startle the group; then a parchment flies out of it and hits the conveyor belt. I exhale as I watch Sasha's story rise up and roll straight for the bright-yellow mirror. Then it disappears in a blast of light.

All that's left to do is get out of here without being caught.

Olivina's eyes narrow as she watches us move to the door. "Ogres. How clever. Prue and Corden's gifts have gotten so much stronger. Hazel, it's the banished students. Call the Dwarf Police Squad at once!"

"Tara?" Olivina calls. "I know you're there! Come home! Please! Don't run!"

"Run!" Tara says, barreling down two RA students on her quest to get past them.

"Seize them!" Hazel spins around, unsure where to go first. "Guards!"

A student behind her bursts into tears as if we might turn them all into a crop of turnips with a wave of our hands. A few start to scream. A buzzer on the door sounds, and I hear an announcement being made about intruders. I look at Hershel's statue and realize there's a door right behind it.

"Over there!" I shout. "GO!"

The five of us don't wait. We dash through just in time to hear it slam firmly behind us.

9

THE GETAWAY PLAN

reat!" Tara complains. A siren in the building begins to wail. "You've led us deeper into the building!"

"Did you have a better idea? Running toward Hazel didn't seem that wise either."

There's still another doorway ahead of us. Through it, I see ogres singing "Happy Birthday" so loudly they must have missed the announcement. Their door seals shut before they can even ask us what's going on. We're trapped in the hallway between both rooms.

"Hey! What are you doing? Hey! We're on lunch break for Gangia's party! Open up!" An ogre pounds on the door.

Behind us, we hear banging as well. "You little cretins!

You've been banished! How did you get into the village? How?" Hazel bellows. "Open the door this instant!"

"My buddy in my ear says there is definitely another exit from this hallway," Heath tells us. "Everyone look." We begin patting the walls and removing the parchments, looking for secret exits, but there's nothing there.

Both doorways are sealed, and there are no windows. The walls are decorated with famous *Happily Ever After Scrolls* posts from years past, most of which feature Olivina's smiling face: The coronation of the royal court. The opening of Fairy Tale Reform School. The ribbon-cutting ceremony at the Enchantasia Zoological Institute of Magical Creatures. There is no way to get away from the fairy godmother. We're trapped.

"Keep looking!" Kira tells me. "It's not on the map, but Prue says there is buzz online about secret passageways used by reviewers trying to flee unhappy restaurant owners, royal seamstresses, and blog writers."

"No surprise there!" Sasha must have just received the same report. She bangs on a piece of molding near the ceiling and tries to pry it loose. "In a roundup of the Kingdom's Creative Creatures, they only gave my blog two wands out of five because I use anonymous sources!"

"The Dwarf Police Squad have arrived at the building and—" Kira stops midsentence and shrieks. "There's reports of harpies in the area," she tells me. "Hurry!"

"Olivina is sending harpies!" Tara repeats, her eyes widening. "I knew this was a bad idea. Why did I listen to you lot? We were safe until you arrived!" She slumps down on the floor, holding her knees. "I can't go back to Royal Academy. I can't." She starts to hyperventilate.

"Wow, Tara's even worse off than me," Logan whispers. "We have to get her out of here."

I move a coffee cart to see if there is a vent or anything beneath it, but all I find is a portrait of Olivina receiving a lifetime achievement award from the royal court. Seeing her face, I feel a surge of anger. I grab at the parchment and rip it right off the wall.

"Look!" Logan shouts. "Devin found the way out!" There's a small red knob on the wall where the scroll was just hanging. We gather around to inspect it.

"The squad is entering the newsroom!" Kira shouts.

"It looks like a button to me," Heath presses it. Nothing happens.

"Keep looking!" Sasha goes back to pounding the wall for weak spots.

"It's not a button," Logan says. "It's a secret dumbwaiter. I had one in my kitchen back home and used it all the time to get from my room to the kitchen in the middle of the night to test out recipes."

Instead of pushing the knob, he turns it counterclockwise twice, then spins it three times to the right. A panel in the wall slides away to reveal a large box the size of a window. Inside there is a pulley system. Logan jumps in. "Come on! There is room for two of us to go up at a time." Sasha climbs in after him. Logan pulls the rope and the box goes flying up. The rest of us look into the shaft and watch the box disappear into the darkness, then hit the top hard. I cringe.

"We're all right!" Logan yell down to us. "Send more!"

"They're at the door!" Kira says. The box zips back down and comes to a halt in front of us.

I see Heath touch his earpiece. "You two in first. I'll take the last run. Go!"

Tara is so upset she can barely move. I help her up and cram her into the dumbwaiter, then climb in after her. The space is tight and feels claustrophobic, like that time I hid in a hollow tree in our gardens when Mother wanted to take me shoe shopping. We start to ascend with alarming speed. I hear Kira's frantic voice in my ear: "They're breaking through! Hurry!"

I roll Tara and myself out of the dumbwaiter, and seconds later, the dumbwaiter rockets back down. I hear it rattling upward just as fast, and to my relief, Heath comes tumbling out. "Close the opening!" he sputters. "They're in the hallway!"

"Stand back." Logan pushes us all out of the way. There is a red button next to our exit. Logan does the reverse of what he did below—spinning the knob in the opposite direction and the shaft looks like a wall again. Logan sighs with relief. "I miss having a dumbwaiter. I hid so many soufflés from my hungry nanny in those."

"No time for stories!" Kira says. "You need to get out of the village Prue says Olivina is calling for barricades."

"Which way do we go?" Heath asks, looking from the dark alley to our left to the busy street filled with carriages and magic carpets on our right.

"One wrong move, and we're done for," Tara says grimly.

I ignore Tara and look for a clue about which way we should go. I spot a small rat and lean down to his level. "Excuse me? Can you give us directions on the quickest way out of here?" I ask, speaking in squeaks and tongue clicks.

The rat looks at me, and his whiskers twitch slightly. "Do not head into the village square. You'll get trampled. Go toward the dark alley. It leads to a residential street of extra-large boot homes. You can get lost in there."

"Thank you, sir!" I wish I had some of that energy bar left to give him. "Into the dark alley!"

Tara looks from the rat to me. "Into the dark alley? That can't be right!"

I hold my chin up high. "This rat knows the village better than anyone, and if he says go toward the alley, I think we should go toward the alley."

"Prue says Olivina is sending more reinforcements, and they're looking for ogres," Kira adds. "Plus, the harpies have entered the village square! You need to get out of your costumes immediately. No one knows your faces as well as they do your disguises. Ditch them."

"Costumes off now," I tell the others. "Kira, tell Prue we'll be heading into the village residential area. We can wait there till the coast is clear, then make our way back to the forest."

"Wait?" Tara repeats. "Out in the open? No. There has to be quicker way! Maybe we can reach Robin Hood with our kobolds." Tara holds her right earlobe. "Tinky? What?" Tara looks at the rest of us. "She can't reach Prue. We've lost contact."

In the distance, I hear another siren and more shouting. This is bad.

"Olivina must have scrambled the signal," Kira tells me. "You need to de-ogre and get out of here!"

We shed our costumes quickly, then rush to the end of the alley, emerging onto a quiet street with boots, houses, and teacups. A few children are playing tag on a lawn, and a magic carpet stand with children selling patty cakes is set up near the street. There's no sign of the Dwarf Police Squad. Tara makes her way to the kids playing tag and snatches one of their cloaks lying on the ground.

"Blend in and follow me. We are getting back to the forest *now*." She wraps the purple cloak around her shoulders.

Sasha, Heath, Logan, and I stick close together and walk swiftly.

"You've got this," Kira coaches me. "A few blocks over is a path that leads to the forest. Just keep your head down… Ooh! Strawberry-rhubarb cookies!"

A group of kids in Mother Goose Nursery School shirts

have just set up a stand to sell cookies. In seconds, a crowd of kids is swarming us, begging for us to buy cookies.

"You need to keep moving," Kira says as I almost get poked in the eye by a piece of cookie a kid is holding over his head. Strawberry sauce oozes down his arm, and he licks it. Gross.

"I'm trying!" I say, and the kid looks at me strangely.

"I swear, kobolds do not get paid enough for this type of stress," Kira mutters.

Heath grabs my arm, and with one sharp tug, I'm loose.

"You're not going to buy any cookies?" one of the kids yells.

"Sorry!" I say sheepishly. We rush to keep up, but Tara and Logan disappear around a corner, and we lose track of them.

"Three more blocks," Kira says. "Keep your eyes down and—*What?*" She shouts in my ear. "Prue? Prue? She just cut back in and vanished again!"

"What's going on?" I ask as Sasha and Heath put their hand to their ears. Two mothers standing on their porch stare at us. My heart stops when I realize they're holding mini magical scrolls.

"It's them!" one of the mothers cries. "Police! Help!"

Whistles sound all around us. One woman runs past us to grab her child from the cookie stand. She drops her mini magical scroll running away. The day's news from *Happily Ever After Scrolls* has disappeared, replaced with portraits of me and my friends. The photos were taken our first day at Royal Academy, but I could swear my awkward smile has been magically replaced with a scowl. Above our portraits it says: WANTED: ROYAL ACADEMY OUTLAWS! *Reward for their capture by direct order of Olivina!*

ROSE-COLORED GLASSES

Within moments of reading the warning, a small man with a flashing Dwarf Police Squad badge appears on horseback. His badge says CHIEF PETE. His eyes narrow. "There they are! Get them!"

"Run!" Sasha shouts.

We almost knock down the nursery-school kids in our haste to get away, but I keep running. We're rounding the corner when we're cut off by a magic carpet ridden by two boys.

"It's them!" shouts one of the boys. "Grab them!"

"This way!" Heath shouts, ducking into a very narrow opening between a boot home and a teakettle. Four trolls greet us halfway down the alley.

"Nice reward for you lot," slurs one.

"Keeps us in good standing with Olivina," says another, drool dripping from his mouth. He advances on us.

I turn around to run and find the entrance we just came down blocked by a mob of people. One way is trolls, the other an angry mob. Who knows what's happened to Tara and Logan. We need another way out. I look down, up, sideways, for dumbwaiter knobs and find nothing. Then I spot an open door to a boot a few feet away.

"You'll have to win favor with the fairy godmother another way!" I shout, sliding through the trolls' legs and into the door.

Heath and Sasha are right behind me. Heath slams the door shut, and I breathe a sigh of relief. I can hear the trolls pounding on the door, but this baby has a dead bolt. Thank the fairies.

"May I help you?" someone asks, and I jump.

I turn around. We're in a shoemaker's shop. Boots hang from the ceiling, glass slippers shine from racks on the wall, and there is a distinct smell of shoe leather. A sign up above the doorway says COBBLER SHOES. A man wearing a very dirty apron walks toward us, looking confused as he shines a boot in his hands.

"Shouldn't you kids be in school?" He smiles. "I've got one about your age. Goes to Fairy Tale Reform School. Any of you go there? You aren't cutting class, are you?"

A siren begins to whirl outside, and we look at one another.

"I..." Sasha begins to say. "We..."

A figure moves out of the shadows. She's dressed in a lilac gown with a skirt made of pink and purple rosebuds, and her hair is long and blond, much like Sasha's. In her hand is a mini magical scroll. She sees us, and her small, round mouth curves into a perfect O.

"Sasha?" The girl rushes toward her. That's when I notice the crown atop her head. "Are you all right? What in the name of Grimm are you doing here?"

Sasha falls into the older girl's arms. "Rose!" She is sobbing so hard it's hard to understand her. "You don't know what's happened. Olivina. Misunderstanding! Harpies. Fake news! Can't trust her! She's. She's. Ev—"

"Shhhhh!" Rose hugs her tighter again as Sasha continues to gulp for air. "Don't worry. Your big sister is here." She glances over Sasha's shoulder at the two of us. "Heathcliff! You're here too? Your sister has been so worried."

"Princess," Heath says with a bow. "We're in a spot of trouble. If you could—"

She cuts him off and looks at me. "And you must be Devinaria, Sasha's roommate." She cocks her head and smiles coyly. "Or should I say former?"

My mouth goes dry. She's Princess Rose of the royal court. "Yes, I—"

There is more pounding on the back door. "Fugitives! Open up! We have you surrounded!"

The shopkeeper looks at Rose. "Princess, if you would like to take your young charges with you, you should leave through the front door at once. I'll hold the others off."

She smiles graciously. "Thank you for understanding, Mr. Cobbler. I'll have my courier pick up my glass slipper order later this week. If anyone asks, you didn't see me."

He bows. "Of course, Princess." He looks at the rest of us. "I know it's hard, but stay out of trouble, littles. As my eldest could tell you, tussling with the Dwarf Police Squad is no picnic."

"Thank you, sir." I follow Sasha and Heath out the front door behind the princess.

Rose's Pegasus carriage is out front. She ushers us inside, then closes the purple curtains to hide us from view.

"Not a word!" she whispers through the veil. "I'm going to speak with our driver to get us out of the village as quickly as possible."

I look at Heath. "What about Logan and Tara? We need to find them."

"They could have been captured," Sasha says worriedly. "Once we get out of here, we can reach Prue and find them. But if we're all captured, we won't do anyone any good."

"But…" I jump when I hear Kira in my ear.

"I can't get word to Prue," she says. "Communication is still down. I'll keep trying."

"We've gotten permission to take off right away." Rose sneaks back into the carriage and squeezes Sasha's hand. "We'll get you out of here. Don't you worry."

Seconds later, the carriage takes off at warp speed.

"We need to get somewhere safe," Sasha tells her. "Could you bring us to Mother and Father first? They'll listen to my side of the story. The fairy godmother doesn't have our best interests at heart. She controls everything in this kingdom and manipulates the students into being mini versions of… well, you!"

Rose's smile fades. "What is wrong with that? As a

princess, it is my duty to serve my people and be someone they look up to. I do not veer from Olivina's chosen path. As a fairy godmother, she knows what's best for each of us, including you. If you'd just see reason."

Sasha pulls away. "See reason?"

"Yes!" Rose tries to take her hand again. "I could speak with Olivina and get her to readmit you if you'd just fall into line like the other students. Stop trying so hard to be different! It makes you look difficult. Why can't you just be more like me?"

Heath gives me a look. Who knew Rose was such an Olivina fangirl? Sasha is her sister! She should believe her.

"Devin!" Kira screams in my ear, and I jump.

"Shh!" I don't want Rose to know she's here.

"More like you?" Sasha turns stone-faced. "You mean like when you joined forces with Gottie and tried to take over Fairy Tale Reform School? Was that your idea or Olivina's?"

"That's enough from you, missy!" Rose's face reddens. "There you go again, acting as if you're so high and mighty. You always had such lofty ideals. I see now why Olivina wanted to shut down that silly blog of yours."

"Devin!" Kira says again, and I feel the carriage begin to lift into the air.

"My blog is not silly! If you read it, you'd know!" Sasha fires back. "It tells the truth, unlike Olivina."

Rose's eyes flash. "Olivina never lies. She knew you were bad seeds. She was right to banish you!" Sasha looks like she's been slapped.

"Devin!" Kira's voice is so loud Heath hears it. "This carriage is headed for Royal Academy!"

"What?" I look at the others. "She's taking us back to Royal Academy!"

Sasha looks at her sister. "Rose? You turned us in?"

Rose falters. "It was the only way. The fairy godmother feels you're all causing too much of a commotion. If you'd just accepted your banishment quietly, maybe you could have been redeemed in the future, but clearly that's not an option now. She needs to speak to you directly, and I'm the one she'll find favor with for bringing you there."

"You really are evil," Sasha spits out.

Heath pulls back the curtain and looks out. We're above the treetops of the village now. "It's too high to jump."

Rose sits back calmly. "You might as well accept it."

"The odds of surviving a jump from this high are slim," Kira says grimly.

My heart is racing as I stick my face out the window. The wind whips at my cheeks. We need to get out of here, but how? My eyes land on the four Pegasi flying the carriage. If I could just get their attention… I look back. Sasha is still arguing with Rose so I give a whistle.

The driver doesn't seem to notice the Pegasus make eye contact with me. All he hears is a neigh. *Yes, miss! How can I help you?*

I'm hoping the wind covers my voice. "Can this fly with only two Pegasi?" I say in neighs. "We need to get out of this carriage right away! We're being held captive!"

Of course, miss! We could fly this thing with one Pegasus, but you know how the royals are. Four Pegasi look better than two, two look better than one… Just climb on up here, and we'll break two Pegasi free.

"Be right there!" I shout, and this time the driver looks back and stares at me strangely. "Sasha, Heath, we're going. Princess…nice meeting you?" I add awkwardly.

"Going? We're in the air," Rose reminds me with a laugh.

"Going?" Kira is shrill. "If you fall from this height, you'll be a pancake! There must be another way."

"There's not." I climb onto the carriage window ledge. Why do I always look down? Instantly, I freeze. It's like I'm back on the tree house plank, sure I'm going to fall, except this time there's no trampoline to catch me.

You can do it! the Pegasi neigh. *Go slowly and hold on to the carriage rails.*

There is a railing that I can hold onto as I shimmy to the driver's seat, and I just need to hold on tight. I hear a commotion in the carriage, but I try not to pay attention.

Heath sticks his head and his arm out and hands me a rope. "Prue gave me this lasso. It will tie itself onto anything you throw it at. The other end will stick magically to your hand. Lasso it onto the driver's seat, and it should keep you from falling off. I'll be right behind you."

Should? I pull myself up to standing. The carriage bounces and my right leg slides off the window ledge. I quickly pull it up. *Deep breath, Devin.* I hold the lasso in my right hand and try to shake it off. It holds firm. That's good! Then I fling the other end at the driver.

It winds itself tightly on the back of the driver's seat without a sound. So far, so good. Slowly, I start to shimmy along the side of the carriage. The carriage bounces again, and I'm now hanging on to the carriage by the lasso.

"Devin!" Heath shouts as we fly through a dark cloud.

The driver turns and sees me hanging off the carriage. "Princess! What are you doing? Get back inside!"

I've only got one shot at this. I push off the carriage with my feet and feel the lasso swing me forward. I land behind the driver and hold on for dear life.

"Help!" he shouts, losing his grip on the reins. The carriage tilts precariously to the right. From inside, I can hear Rose scream. The driver pulls on the reins again, and the carriage rights itself again. I step over his seat before he knows what's happening and climb onto the Pegasus.

"Oh my word, we're alive!" Kira shouts, then bursts into tears in my ear.

Nice job, Princess! the Pegasus says.

"Thanks!" I turn around, unwinding the lasso from my grip and flinging it back for Heath to grab. He starts moving right away.

"We need to make an emergency landing!" the driver tells the footman seated next to him.

"Princess Rose said keep going at all costs!" the footman says. "Olivina's orders."

As the clouds break, I see the peaks of Royal Academy in the distance.

Heath shimmies toward me and the footman tries to grab him from behind.

"Watch out!" I shout, and Heath kicks him away.

This isn't going to work a second time. "I'm going to unhook us from the carriage," I tell the Pegasus. "We need to pick up two more passengers. Heath!" I shout. "Wait there!"

"Where would I go?" Heath is hanging off the side of the carriage, bouncing around like a magic bean. I can't risk him falling off.

Yes, Princess! Go for it! my Pegasus tells me as I unwind the knots holding them to the carriage. Rose and the drivers will be fine. The other two Pegasi will stay attached, but the front two are soon free. One flaps its large wings and turns around to grab Heath, who climbs on his back.

"Do something!" I hear the footman shout. I fly off behind Heath's Pegasus, who is now hovering near the window of the carriage where Rose and Sasha are arguing. Sasha sees me and does a double take.

Rose sticks her head out in alarm. "What are you doing?" she screams. "You're going to fall!"

"Jump!" I say.

Sasha looks back at her sister for a moment, then climbs

through the window, pulling herself on behind me before Rose even realizes what's happening.

"Stop them!" Rose shouts to the driver and the footman, but they're too busy trying to fly the carriage with two fewer Pegasi. Rose looks back at us as we start to pull away. "No! Sasha! Don't!" Rose screams, but her voice is snatched away by the wind as the two Pegasi carry us off into the afternoon clouds, blocking us from sight.

~~Happily Ever After Scrolls~~

The Enchantasia Insider

The Real Kingdom News

Greetings, royal lovers! Did you miss me?

I apologize for my unplanned absence. I know it seemed awfully rude of me to vanish before writing about Countess Claudette's long-awaited wedding to the Prince of Sandringham (Oh, the swan-boat procession! The singing lobsters! The firefly fireworks spectacular! This couple truly likes to celebrate in the grandest of styles!), but sometimes princesses really do have to abandon their glass slippers before the stroke of midnight.

This happened to be one of those times, and the change of footwear was not my choice.

You see, I, along with several of my classmates, was banished from Royal Academy. I know it's not in my nature to share details about my true identity, but desperate times call for desperate measures. The sad truth, my royal lovers, is that the atmosphere at Royal Academy is toxic, and the truth must be brought to light.

From the outside, Royal Academy may appear dreamlike, but appearances can be different from reality.

Consider the enrollment process: If you're born royal, you must attend this school, which is run by our kingdom's most trusted fairy godmother. But this fairy godmother is no godsend. In truth, she rules the school to fulfill her own agenda. By controlling what young princes and princesses learn and who they will someday become, she can ensure that they rule this kingdom the way *she* sees fit.

By forcing students to take the classes she believes they should take, she prevents students from reaching their true potential, whether that's becoming a culinary genius or a journalist like myself. By teaching students to fear those who are different (i.e., not royal), she is ensuring they follow an elitist path rather than learn about the people they are meant to rule. And what of the rule that only royalty should sit upon a throne? What if the right person for the job does not have a royal pedigree? Should they be overlooked because of their lack of title? We think not! Just as Fairy Tale

Reform School has taught us a villain can be redeemed, we must also accept that a beloved fairy godmother could have darker motives.

I urge my readers to open their eyes and ears and question what they know about Royal Academy's headmistress. My friends and I were banished from Royal Academy last week, not for committing any sort of villainy, but for exposing the truth about her nefarious intentions. But we won't let the fairy godmother continue to endanger the citizens of Enchantasia. We urge you to rise up and express your concerns with us. Not just for us, but for the good of all our people!

More soon…

Signed: Sasha Briarwood, with Heathcliff White, Raina White, Logan Nederlander, and Devinaria Nile

PARTY POOPER

So remember, Nigel," I say as the Pegasus swoops lower over the trees in the forest, looking for the pirate-ship tree house. "When you feel a bout of tummy troubles coming on, chew some mint leaves. It settles the stomach just like that!" I snap my fingers.

Nigel neighs in agreement. *Thanks for the tip, Devinaria. And I'm sorry you're having all this trouble with Fairy Godmother Olivina. All I know is she's restricted the airspace over the school. We aren't allowed to fly in or out without her written permission. This is the first time in fifteen years she's done that! Something strange is brewing. You steer clear.*

"I will, Nigel, and take care of Penelope," I add, referencing his Pegasus partner in crime who helped us escape

Princess Rose. "I don't want you two getting in trouble with the royal court."

We won't, Nigel neighs as we descend below the tree line toward the pirate ship. *We're friends with the Pegasi at Fairy Tale Reform School. I'm sure they'll let us stay there until things calm down. They'll keep us safe.*

I hear a whistle and see Prue waving to us from the crow's nest. She's shouting something I can't hear. I squint harder and realize she's not alone.

Fairy be, Logan is standing next to her, peering at us with one big brown eye through a telescope! They're okay!

Nigel comes in for a landing on the deck, and Tara comes running toward us.

"What happened to you guys?" she says angrily.

So much for a warm welcome.

"I told you to stick right behind us!"

Sasha dismounts behind me. "We got lost in the crowd when the warning appeared on the scrolls."

"You *should* have walked faster! What if Olivina had grabbed us?" Tara scolds.

"Thankfully, we got away." Sasha pats Nigel. "Thanks for rescuing us." Nigel neighs.

"He says it was his honor," I translate for Sasha, ignoring Tara. "And he says no matter what your sister says, you're a true princess."

Tara's eyes bulge. "You saw Princess Rose?"

Sasha smiles sadly. I don't blame her. I don't know how I'd feel if I had a sister who tried to betray me.

Penelope lands with a thud next to Nigel, and Heath jumps off. "Everyone all right?" He pulls at his ear, letting his kobold climb out. Sasha and I do the same.

"Yes, but Logan and I barely got away," Tara says. "He's not the quickest on foot."

"Hey, if it weren't for my suggestion that we jump in those water barrels and roll down the hill, we might not have made it to Red and Prue without being spotted." Logan looks at me in awe. "It was amazing! Red was waiting in the forest, and she shot arrows with smoke at the police horses to keep them back. None of the horses were hurt," he tells me hurriedly. "But the smoke kept us from sight. When we didn't see you three, I thought something bad had happened."

"It did," Heath recounts our run-in with Rose.

"You told Rose about us?" Tara says shrilly.

"We didn't say anything about you! But even if we had,

Olivina already knows you're out here," I remind her. "She's the one that banished you. Who cares if Rose knows too?"

"You don't get it! The more noise we make, the harder it gets for us to survive. We've made a home out here, and if your plan doesn't work with *HEAS*, you're going to ruin it for us!"

I am flabbergasted. "This is a hideout. Not your home. Don't you miss your family?"

Tara's finger almost jabs my nose. "You don't get it. I'm willing to sacrifice having a normal life if it means keeping everyone safe!"

Prue steps in between us. "Let's all calm down. Everyone is safe. The scroll is in. Now we've got a real shot at reversing this banishment and setting things right at the school. Isn't that what we really want? To get out of this forest?"

Tara doesn't answer. "I'll be on lookout. We need to be ready if Rose trailed you guys here." Tara grabs a rope from the ship deck, flips a switch, and gets pulled up to the crow's nest.

Corden and Prue look at each other. Prue shakes her head. "Sometimes I still forget all Olivina took from her."

"What do you mean?" Sasha asks.

"This is the only home Tara has left," Prue says. "That's why she's so comfortable out here. She was an orphan before

Olivina invited her to come to RA. While she was there, Tara learned her mother was destroyed under Olivina's rule. So she ran. She made her own family out here, and she doesn't want to lose it now."

"When Prue and I got banished here, Tara was all alone," Corden explains. "She had been for some time. She's rough around the edges, but she takes care of all of us like our very own fairy godmother would."

"I didn't realize," I say softly.

"It's okay," Prue says. "Let's just give her some space. We've got work to do. With your *HEAS* post, Olivina will be sending more gargoyles into the forest—or worse. I better put up some defense charms."

I look at Tara up in the crow's nest and feel a lump in my throat. At least when I was banished, I had my friends. Tara had to make it on her own until she found Corden and Prue. No wonder she's not in any rush to give up the family she created.

"Speaking of family, has anyone seen Raina?" Heath asks.

Corden picks up a box of handheld mirrors and grimaces. "She's still in front of the mirror. I couldn't pull her away."

We walk past Prue's mirrors that show feeds of the village and the Dwarf Police Squad headquarters. Chief Pete is standing on a table shouting. I suspect it's about us getting away. Raina is sitting in the same position where we left her. She's cross-legged with her chin in her hands, and she's glued to the mirror's feed of Royal Academy. The dark circles under her eyes make me think she still hasn't slept.

"Raina?" I wave my hand in front of her face. "Aren't you tired? How about a nap?"

Raina barely looks up from a mirror showing a group of princesses walking with books on their heads. In another mirror, princes are perfecting their sword-fighting techniques. A third mirror shows Olivina's empty office and her hot-pink velvet chair.

"I don't feel like a turkey leg, right now, thank you," Raina mumbles.

I look at the others strangely. "Um, we weren't talking about food."

"Let me try. Maybe you just need to say what she wants to hear." Logan steps in front of Raina, blocking her view of the mirror. "Raina! You won the most Royal Academy superlatives ever!"

"Thank you, pink is my signature color," she says in a monotone voice.

"I'm so sorry," Corden says to us. "It's easy to get hooked on the mirrors. I did for a spell myself because Marta Marigold is a genius at makeovers. You can't look away from her in the Royal Underground! But then I realized, why watch someone else do what I want to do myself?"

Prue rolls her eyes. "Here you go again, knocking progress. Think of how much these mirrors show us. They've been the best protection we have."

"Look at what they've done to Raina," Corden argues.

"Can you set a time limit for watching?" Sasha asks.

Prue scratches her chin. "I never thought of doing that. I could probably program one of the wands to set a timer for too much viewing, but I don't have that set up right now."

"Can you disconnect them?" Heath tries.

"I could, but there's always the risk they will change the security protocol and I won't be able to get a live feed of RA again."

"Can you *fake* shutting them off?" Heath suggests.

Prue nods, smiling slightly. "That I can do." She taps a

few things on a mini mirror in her hands and the screens all go dark.

"*Hey!*" Raina jumps up immediately. "I was watching that! Prue! The mirrors went dark! *Prue!*" She spins around and sees us all standing there. "Oh, there you are. Prue, the mirrors have… Hey, why are you guys so dirty? Did you go somewhere?"

I look at the clothes I had on under my ogre costume. They're sweaty, stained, and I have leather polish on my arm sleeve from something I brushed up against in Cobbler Shoes. My hair may have a few leaves in it too.

"What is going on here?"

"We went to the *Happily Ever After Scrolls* offices so Sasha could secretly post a blog about Olivina's motives and try to get our banishment lifted," Heath explains. "You were too busy watching your mirrors to join us."

"What? If you go after Olivina, she'll never lift our banishment!" Raina sounds aghast.

"She will if we expose her true intentions," Sasha argues. "I signed all of our names to my blog post to give it more weight. I'm sure that's why Rose is so angry with me."

Raina's eyes nearly bulge out of her head. "Rose knows?"

"If the royal court questions Olivina, she'll fight back hard and wand us into oblivion. Where will this end? We'll never stop fighting with Olivina, and we'll never get home!"

"Is that what you want?" Heath asks. "To go home and live our lives the way the fairy godmother sees fit? Watch Snow be manipulated by her along with the rest of the royal court?"

Raina purses her lips. "Of course not! But not everything Olivina proposes is bad. I like parties and superlatives and learning how to handle my duties as a royal."

"And what duties are those?" Sasha fires back. "To wear a pretty crown while sitting on a throne of Olivina's choosing? We should have a say in who we want to be. Olivina shouldn't decide for us."

"I think we should all cool off," Corden says, and I nod in agreement. The others aren't listening.

"There's nothing wrong with wanting some things to stay the same!" Raina disagrees.

Heath looks angry. "You mean like following the Royal Academy rules and going to balls? All of that stuff is useless, Raina!"

Raina pokes him in the chest. "Take that back!"

"Make me!" Heath folds his arms across his chest.

"That's enough!" I squeeze between them. "We can't turn on one another."

"You're right," Heath says with a sigh. "I don't want to fight."

"Me either." Raina plops down on a box, her beautiful blue silk skirt billowing around her. "But Heath is right," she says, looking up at me with tear-filled eyes. "I was so busy watching the mirrors that I missed the quest. Not that I would have been much help anyway. I don't know how to do this revolutionary stuff. I can't help it if I was *good* at being a royal but I'm totally out of my element here in the woods. There aren't any balls to attend or rankings to win. I don't fit in anywhere."

Heath puts a hand on her shoulder. "You belong here with us."

"Not really," she says sadly. "I'm here by default because I blabbed to Olivina, thinking it would get us out of a jam. I'm not brave like Sasha or quick on my feet like Devin or resourceful like Logan." She looks up at her brother. "Even you are good with a map and a leading an expedition. But me? I don't have anything to offer outside Royal Academy." Her lower lip quivers.

"That's not true," I say gently. "You're one of the kindest, most graceful people I've ever met. You can navigate any social situation with ease, and you command any room you walk into. I don't know about you, but I think those are pretty useful skills."

Raina looks up at me with a watery smile.

I hear a thump, and we all jump. Tara has landed back on the deck. "Shh!" she hisses. "We've got company!"

ENCHANTASIA'S MOST WANTED

My skin starts to tingle. I feel Lily wiggling in my pocket and know she feels the same thing. Something is coming. I smell it before I can even see it in the growing darkness. It smells like pond water that has sat still too long, or a skunk who sprayed a squirrel during an argument. I crawl toward the railing of the tree house to get a better look.

Prue hits some buttons on her mirrors and the shield goes back up, but I am not sure she's in time. We duck down behind one of Corden's large wardrobe trunks and try not to breathe as a flock of gargoyles flies into view. Their high-pitched shrieks nearly pop my eardrums as they zip right by the tree house without even pausing.

"They missed us." Logan breathes a sigh of relief and starts to rise.

Look out!" Prue cries.

A gargoyle swoops over the deck and tosses a burning scroll onto it. The scroll unfurls, lighting the deck on fire. I catch a quick glimpse of it as it turns to ash.

It's a WANTED poster. And it's for all of us.

Another burning scroll lands near it. It's Sasha's *Enchantasia Insider* post. The words YOU CAN'T WIN are written over it in bright red.

"The deck is on fire!" Raina shouts. To my surprise, she runs to one of Corden's trunks and pulls out a pink satin shoe. She weighs it in her hand for a moment, then takes aim at a gargoyle, spiky heel first. The shoe comes dangerously close to the creature's wing. It shrieks and flies higher, dropping the next flaming scroll in its grasp.

"The whole tree house is going to go up!" Prue frantically tries wanding the broken shield.

Heath shoots an arrow that narrowly misses a gargoyle. Several more scrolls hit the tree house deck, covering the floor in smoke.

"Stop! Please! Stop!" I beg, but the gargoyles keep

attacking. I can't tell if they can see us or they just know where we are.

I hear a loud shriek. Raina has made a direct hit to one's wing. I feel bad as it shrieks in pain, but it does the trick. Seconds later, the gargoyles take off into the night.

We try stomping out small fires all around the deck, but it keeps growing.

I look around for something to put out the flames. Logan runs by me with a large, blue parasol.

"Stand back!" he shouts. He opens it up as if he's expecting rain and pulls a lever on the hook. White foam shoots out of the parasol, covering the flames and putting them out. He runs around the deck with his umbrella until all that's left are a few smoking patches.

Logan collapses onto a barrel bench and looks at us. "I always carry one of these Rainy Day Insurance Umbrellas in my pocket. It triples in size in seconds and can be used in a rainstorm to prevent a lightning strike or to put out a fire. Red Riding Hood invented it." He gives me a knowing look. "Very handy if you have a grease fire in the kitchen."

Corden high-fives him. "Nice job, mate."

Logan beams. "Thanks! I've never saved the day before.

I thought that sort of thing only happened when you slayed a giant or a beast."

"Me too!" Raina says, eyeing the glittery pump in her hand with awe. "That felt good."

"I wouldn't start celebrating yet." Tara picks up the charred remains of a scroll. "Our blog post was canceled.

"That's impossible!" Sasha cries."

Prue taps the small mirror in her hand and frowns. "She's right. The post is down. Look."

We gather around. The post is not on the day's feed as it should be.

"It looks like it was only up for maybe thirty minutes at most." Prue holds her head. "What a waste."

"Guys," I hear Raina say.

"No one even saw it!" says Tara, getting upset. "We risked being captured, exposing the tree house and our anonymity, and for what? Olivina still wins!" She looks at me. "I told you this would happen! She's too powerful. Maybe the best thing we can do is stay in the shadows so none of us get hurt. She can't be stopped."

"But she needs to be," I press.

"Not if it means we lose the ones we love," Tara counters.

"Guys, look!" Raina speaks up. She uses her shoe to point to one of the mirrors at Royal Academy. Olivina is in her office, and she's talking to a group of very upset people.

"It's our parents," I realize. We crowd around the mirror.

My father is in his royal infantry uniform, his gold sash adorned with too many medals to count. He's standing next to my tearful mother, who keeps sneaking glances at Snow (who practically raised Heath and Raina, from what I've heard). There's also another couple who must be Sasha's parents. She looks exactly like her father.

"Can someone turn the mirror up?" Tara asks.

"...has gone too far!" I hear my father thunder. "First you banish our children without any word, and now we find out they're being hunted? How do you explain this?"

"Commander Nile, there is no need to get upset," Olivina says with a pleasant smile. "Your children are perfectly safe. I know exactly where they are."

The hair on the back of my neck stands up.

"You do?" Sasha's mother dabs at her eyes with a paisley-print handkerchief that matches her gown.

"Of course! I would never abandon any of our young royals, even when they do something that deserves punishment. Once they've repented for their behavior, they are welcome back at Royal Academy."

"So the banishment isn't a true banishment?" Snow asks. "Because according to this article Sasha published in *Happily Ever After Scrolls*—"

"I thought that post was taken down," Olivina says to Hazel quickly.

"It was," Hazel says, looking fearful. "It was only up for thirty minutes."

"Well, I read it," Snow tells them, "and, according to Sasha, they aren't the first group to be banished. Does that mean you've located the others, including Tara?"

I notice Tara's face harden.

"Tara's family knows I know what's best for her."

But I thought Tara had no family?

"She can't be a fine ruler unless she learns how to follow the rules, now can she? Just like Sasha." Olivina tsks. "Airing our royal dirty laundry like that is a no-no. Very hurtful."

"But what she wrote, was it the truth?" Sasha's father asks. "Are you manipulating the royals in this kingdom to do your bidding?"

Olivina looks aghast. "Of course not!" She motions to

her couch. "Please, let's all sit down and chat." She holds up a tray of baked goods. "Try one of these chocolate rhubarb muffins I just got the recipe for. You'll feel so much better."

"Thank you, Fairy Godmother." Snow takes a bite of a muffin. "I don't mean to question your judgment. It's just we're having trouble understanding what our siblings and children could have done that deserved banishment in the first place. You've been a part of my family for years. If my brother and sister were not following school protocol, I should have been notified. We all should have been... Oh. What did you say was in these? Rhubarb?" She takes another bite. "They're delicious!"

"Are they?" Sasha's mother reaches for one. "Our family has had such heartache this year with Rose. If Sasha wasn't upholding her royal duties, shouldn't we, her parents, be the ones to handle that? We've spoken to Logan Nederlander's parents as well. They're actually out searching for their son as we speak, which is why they didn't join us this evening."

"They are?" Logan pipes up. "Wow, and at night too. My parents never go anywhere under the cover of darkness without my brother nearby. Too many things could eat you."

"These are delicious," Sasha's mom says and offers the

plate to my parents. My mother takes one, but my father waves it away.

Olivina folds her hands in her expansive lap, her ruby-red gown fanning out in front of her. "I understand all of you are upset. How do you think I feel? To lose such promising young students so early in their education? It's unheard of! But the path they were going down was too dark to allow it to continue. Try as I might to straighten them out, their behavior led me to believe..." She hesitates and looks at Hazel, who puts an arm on her shoulder. "They were on their way to becoming villains."

Raina is aghast. "How could she say that about us? It's not true!"

"Do you really think so?" Snow asks with a dreamy look on her face.

"Oh dear," says Sasha's mother. "That makes me sad, but if you say so..."

"What's wrong with them?" Heath asks. "Why are they going along with Olivina?"

"I know how hard this is to hear." Olivina's eyes fill up with tears. "But it is the truth! I swear on my fairy godmother code of honor." My mother hands her a handkerchief.

"Thank you, darling. This is all so upsetting. I never like to lose a student under my watch. But the truth is, there is a reason we do things a certain way here."

"These truly are wonderful," my mother says and giggles. "I must get the recipe!"

My father looks at her strangely. "Are you all right?"

"Delightful!" Mother says. "But I do wonder… Oh, what was I wondering? Oh! Yes! Why not just send them to Fairy Tale Reform School then?"

Olivina's smile waffles. "We don't do that here. We already lost one royal to *that school*, and I don't like the idea of royals being mixed in with such…unseemly individuals. We take care of our own. The world is a dangerous place, and I am here to see to it that we're doing things properly so the kingdom has a bright future." She looks at Snow. "Did I not guide you and your fellow royal court?"

"Of course, Fairy Godmother!" Snow agrees.

She turns to Sasha's parents. "Have I not helped end sleeping curses and found cures?"

"Yes!" Sasha's parents reply.

She turns to my parents. "Have your fairy-tale dreams not come true?"

"Indeed, they have," my mother replies.

"Something's wrong," I realize.

"What was in that muffin mix?" Logan asks. "If Olivina made them, maybe there's something in them that is making everyone agreeable when they normally wouldn't be." He taps his chin. "I wonder what she used…"

Raina clutches her chest. "She wouldn't. Would she?"

"We understand now, don't we?" Snow says, and the others mutter in agreement as they take their second or third muffins from the tray.

"No."

"I'm sorry?" I hear Olivina say.

My father steps forward.

"Wanting to be an creature caretaker is not criminal or villainous," my father says even as my mother tries to shush him. "If that's what my Devin did to deserve banishment, then I disagree. I second-guessed sending her here in the first place. She is meant to be a creature caretaker, and I won't let you ruin that just because she wanted that more than she wanted the life you planned for her."

I feel a lump form in my throat. My father is standing up for me.

"Commander Nile, don't be so upset!" Olivina says. "Are you sure you wouldn't like a muffin?"

"No, thank you," he says. "The truth is, I never wanted to pigeonhole my daughter into a life she didn't want. I taught her to be kind, brave, and true to herself, and if that's not enough to make her worthy of her title, then maybe I don't want her to have one."

"That does make sense," Snow holds her head. "I feel so strange, but I agree with the commander. Not everyone born royal is best suited to rule. Raina has always taken to the royal life, but my brother is an expert trailsman and I always thought he'd be a wonderful explorer. Maybe we shouldn't force them into lives they aren't meant to live."

"Whatever Olivina says, I agree with," Sasha's mother argues, and her father sticks a whole muffin in his mouth.

"Mother, fight like Snow!" Sasha shouts at the mirror.

Olivina flashes a tight smile that doesn't quite reach her eyes. "Well, I think that's enough talking for one day." Hazel ushers everyone to the door and takes away the remaining muffins that Sasha's mom is trying to dump in her purse. "Thank you so much for coming in, and do send a Pegasus Post if you hear anything that feels wrong. The media, as you know, can be so one-sided. I don't put much trust in it." Hazel nods in agreement. "And, as I said, if you hear from your children and they choose to follow our ways, I can find it in my heart to welcome them back and remove their banishment."

"Thank you, Fairy Godmother," my mother gushes. "I'm sure they'll agree to come back!"

"But this scroll…" My father tries again.

Olivina waves him away. "Let's hope for the best. Who knows? They might even be back in time for our masquerade ball! Wouldn't that be lovely? Now if you excuse me, I do have a school to run. Thank you so much for coming. And don't forget to take your complimentary copy of my book, *Cursed Childhood: How to Avoid Being a Target for Sleeping Curses and Poison Apples*, on your way out." She waves. "Till we see each other again. And I do hope it's soon!" She laughs gaily until Hazel closes the door behind them. Then her smile fades. "We need to make sure none of those children ever return to Royal Academy."

Hazel writes something down. "But even the other parents have been calling. The ones from last year too. Even someone who knows that Tara girl."

"I don't care! Make sure, Hazel. I mean it." Olivina's eyes darken. "I'll find a way to push Snow off the scent. Rose is on board, of course. We don't need anyone messing with our plans." She begins to pace. "We will dazzle them all at the masquerade ball, and this talk of misfits and outlaws will be forgotten. I am sure of it."

"And if not?" Hazel asks.

"Then we will find a way to deal with the parents too." Olivina walks away from the screen.

Around me, the only sounds I hear are crickets and an occasional owl. The gargoyles are gone. The last of the fire is out except for a few flaming embers. We stare at the empty mirror in disbelief.

Logan starts to laugh loopily. "Well, guess we're never going home now. Have you all ever thought of putting an extension on the tree house? Because if I'm staying here, I'd like a well-equipped kitchen."

"We're not staying here, are we?" Raina asks, the worry in her voice mounting.

I slump down, feeling defeated again. The scroll didn't stick. Our parents couldn't get through to Olivina. I wonder where Logan's firebird feather is right now, because at the moment, I'm starting to think it really was a bad omen.

"Where else would we go?" Heath asks.

Raina turns to the mirror again. I'm worried she's going to sink back into her stupor. Instead, she touches her hand to the glass, then looks back at us. "Wouldn't it be great if that conversation between Hazel and Olivina could be replayed? But mirrors don't do that, I guess. They show the here and now." She looks at Prue. "Right?"

Prue opens her mouth and closes it several times, reminding me of a bullfrog that is having trouble catching flies. (It's all in the right tongue flick.) "I haven't tried to do that before, but that doesn't mean it couldn't work. I wish I knew how to do it right now."

"And I wish we knew more about this masquerade ball," Corden cuts in. "It hasn't been mentioned on the mirrors before now. Can you imagine what Marta is cooking up for those dresses? I would make the most epic masks. Not just eye masks. Full-face masks with feathers. And pearls and… well, great disguises."

And that's when an idea begins to form. "Maybe we don't have to convince the kingdom that Olivina is up to no good," I say slowly. "Maybe she can out herself."

Corden smiles. "That masquerade ball they talked about would be the perfect cover."

"We could go in, hack into the mirror, and share the truth about Olivina with the whole kingdom!" Heath says excitedly.

Sasha nods. "She wouldn't be able to stop us this time."

Prue slowly smiles. "If we got to the mirror in Olivina's office, we could tap into the connection and share it with more mirrors. I think I could figure out how to do it in a few days."

"You want to go back to Royal Academy?" Tara seems to fold into herself, retreating into the shadows of the darkened ship.

"Yes." I take her hand. "I know it's scary, but she's putting the whole kingdom in danger, and we're the only ones who know."

"Think about all of the other kids out there like us whose lives Olivina wants to destroy," Logan adds. "She could take away their families too."

"We need to fight for them and ourselves, and we need to do it together." I look down at Lily who flicks her tongue in agreement.

"It's risky," Sasha says. "But what can she really do? Banish us again?"

"Send us to Fairy Tale Reform School?" Raina asks

somewhat hopefully. "Azalea and Dahlia—the formerly wicked stepmother's daughters—said it's not all that bad. And if Beauty can work there…"

Tara closes her eyes. "I can't face Olivina again."

"You won't have to do it alone," Heath reminds her.

"We will be there every step of the way." Prue touches her arm.

"We just have to figure out how to get an invitation so we can get through the door," Logan says.

"Lucky for us, we have someone on the inside at Royal Academy," I remind the others. "We just have to send word to her." I walk to the edge of the deck and whistle a call for help in pigeon. A feathered friend flutters down from a nearby tree and lands on the railing. We whistle back and forth. I'm ready to give the bird a snack and send it on its way when Prue runs over.

"If you're getting in touch with a friend at Royal Academy, send her this." She presses a small pink compact mirror into my hand. "You're right. It's time I trust my inventions and give this baby a whirl. I think I can rig it so we can talk to her outside the network at Royal Academy. It should be completely untraceable."

"It's going to work," I say with a smile. Minutes later, my new pigeon friend is on his way to Royal Academy with a note to Brynn and the small compact in tow.

ROYAL ACADEMY

From the desk of the Fairy Godmother

The night has come;

the anticipation is clear.

It's time for our school to show

some goodwill and cheer!

Don your finest threads.

Put on a beautiful mask.

The masquerade ball is here at last!

⋄⋄⋄⋄⋄⋄⋄

While the royal court and esteemed kingdom leaders are invited to attend, this event is only open to royals. Students will be graded on proper attire, costume originality, dance choreography, and how they follow the rules set forth in the Royal Academy Rules. Any questions? Do not bother the fairy godmother! She's too busy. Please see her assistant, Hazel Crooksen.

CHAPTER 13

RIDE OR DIE TRYING

Everything is going to be great!" Prue tucks us into the pumpkin coach taking us to Royal Academy. "Just listen to your kobolds this time!"

"I'll say," Kira says, getting settled in my ear canal. "I thought we were toast last time."

"And if we lose contact, don't try to be a hero. Get out of there." Prue wands her mini magic mirror in front of her. "I have no idea how long this connection will hold up. If you lose me, just remember: swap out one of the jewels in the largest mirror in Olivina's office for this one, and I should be able to tap into the feed." She pulls an ordinary-looking pink jewel from her witch's cape. "Whatever you do, don't lose this. It was extremely hard to create."

I extend one gloved hand to take the jewel, then stash it safely in my pocket. Then I pull out the small compact Prue gave me earlier and open it to make sure it still works. My RA lady-in-waiting's smiling face stares back at me. "Hi, Brynn. Are we still good?"

"Yes, miss!" Her sweet voice comes through loud and clear. She adjusts her white cap and looks around before speaking further. "Make sure you land in the meadow outside the pumpkin patch, and I'll be there to let you all in through the kitchen. No one will be in there this evening."

Prue truly is a genius. Not only did she make that carriage and create the jewel that should let us spy on Olivina, but her mini compact has allowed us to converse with Brynn inside Royal Academy all week. While Corden sewed, and the rest of us plotted, Prue and Brynn made sure we knew exactly what was going on inside the school. Thanks to Brynn, we've scored an official invitation for Princess Scarlet from the kingdom of Lancaster, who is considering transferring to Royal Academy. Brynn slipped the princess's transfer papers and a dossier on Scarlet's "highly promising pedigree" into Hazel Crooksen's clipboard. Olivina was so excited at the prospect of her new student that she handwrote Scarlet's invitation personally.

We've been working really hard to have everything ready in time for tonight.

Raina has made the biggest comeback.

All week, she's refused to sit down in front of the mirrors for fear she'll be sucked back in. Instead, she's been advising Corden on the latest RA fashion trends and even helped him sew the costumes.

When it came time to figure out who should be our "Princess Scarlet," Tara was worried Olivina would spot her from a mile away. Raina was nervous she'd screw up, and I didn't think I was the best choice either, so we agreed it should be Sasha. Raina has been filling her in on everything going on at school (that she's learned from the mirror). Now Sasha can speak intelligently on various topics such as the art of sitting like a lady and how to politely excuse herself from a conversation. I'll admit that last one could be helpful.

I turn back to the pink compact and talk to Brynn. "When the coach gets onto the grounds of RA, Tara and I will make our way to the castle where we'll meet you. In the meantime, the coach will take Sasha and Heath—I mean Princess Scarlet and Prince Edgar—to the front of the castle to join the processional." We've gone over the plan a million times, but I'm still anxious. What if we get caught? What if we can't get into Olivina's office?

Brynn's smile eases my worries for the moment. "I remember, miss! It will be lovely to see you again." Her smile fades. "You have no idea how awful it is being Clarissa's lady-in-waiting. She expects nightly foot rubs because she insists on wearing five-inch glass heels all day." She leans closer into the mirror. "And her feet smell."

This makes me giggle.

"Okay, enough chatting. Let's go already," Tara says as she climbs into the carriage next to me. She's unrecognizable in an ivory gown glittering with small, crystal beans and long, black hair that she dyed with a vegetable rinse Corden made. Corden wanted us all to blend rather than stand out, so he said he didn't go overboard, but I'd say he outdid himself.

"See you soon. And thank you," I tell Brynn. I tuck Lily into my pocket even though she's getting too big for it. She's grown so much now that she's spending so much time out-doors. Then I adjust my wig (I'm now a redhead), and climb in after Tara, being careful not to rip any of the feathers on my skirt.

Heath, Logan, and Sasha are already waiting in the

carriage. Sasha is wearing a bright-green gown that looks lovely with her newly light-brown hair. Heath and Logan have on double-breasted ivory jackets and royal-blue pants that are tucked into over-the-knee black boots. Swords, which I hope we won't have to use, hang from sheaths at their waists.

"Don't forget me!" Raina yells before stepping into the coach. We all inhale sharply. She looks splendid in a pale-blue gown that is embroidered with every color of the rainbow. The stitches swirl in an iridescent sheen that travels up to her hair, which is now curly blond and held back by a feather headband that matches her mask.

"You look unrecognizable," I marvel.

"I know!" She can't suppress her glee. "I love it. It's so freeing not being me! And, you're so right about this, Devin." She lifts her skirt to reveal purple polka-dot pants underneath. Sasha, Tara, and I have the same ones. "Pants make dresses so much more comfortable! How have I never tried them before?"

Ready to go, Devin? asks the Pegasus at the helm. Nigel was able to talk to the Pegasi at the Royal Academy stables, and there were two (Boxer and Ronald) that have a beef with Olivina and were happy to give us an assist.

"Yes, take it away, boys!" I neigh back, gripping the seat in nervous excitement.

The coach begins to bounce along, and in seconds we're taking off into the sky. I look out the window and see Prue and Corden waving from the tree house. We are officially on our way! I turn to the others to find Tara looking green.

"It's going to be all right," I tell her. "We'll keep each other safe."

Tara sighs. "That's what you think."

Sasha unfurls the action-plan scroll in front of her. "Let's go over this one more time. The coach drops us off near the pumpkin patch, where Brynn will sneak us in a back way. Then it takes off and brings Heath and me to the front where we will be presented to Olivina. The voice changer Corden built into our costumes will make sure no one recognizes us. I am Scarlet, an exchange student hoping to attend RA because I've heard great things about Olivina, blah, blah, blah."

Heath turns to the rest of us. "When we get inside, we fan out. Logan will find out when Olivina is going to be arriving at the party. Don't get distracted by what's happening in the kitchen, just find out when her office will be empty. Then have your kobold let our kobolds know. We'll blend in with the party till the coast is clear, then make our way to the office to plant the jewel. Once it's attached to the mirror, we make our way back to the rendezvous point by the kitchen, and then we are out of here. Got it?"

"I don't think I should have come," Tara says quietly. "I'm going to give us away."

"Don't be ridiculous! Corden and Prue have thought of everything!" Logan plays with the scarf tied around his neck. "Even I'm not too worried about being recognized. It's not like many people talked to me at school the first time around anyway."

"You don't get it," Tara starts to say, but stops herself when she sees my compact is glowing.

I open it up and see Brynn again. "Coast is clear!" she says. "The sooner you get here, the better."

"I think we're getting close," I spy the castle's turrets through the carriage windows. "Kira?" I ask my kobold. "Check with Prue to see if it's time for the descent."

I hear a lot of neighing coming from the front of the carriage and wonder what's going on. Our coach hits a few air bumps, and we bounce around for a moment, then level out.

"Prue says it's time!" Kira's voice is so loud over the wind that I hold my ears. "Descend! Descend fast! Now! Now! Now!"

I hear frantic neighing again, and the carriage bounces around some more, dropping slowly.

"What's going on?" Logan shouts. "Is this normal?"

I try to lean out of the carriage to talk to the Pegasi, but another bounce sends me flying backward into Heath. The carriage starts to drop rapidly.

"We're going too fast!" he shouts over the commotion. The Pegasi neighs have grown louder. Raina clings to Heath's arm while I hang on to the other. Sasha, Tara, and Logan are hanging on to the other side of the carriage for dear life. I look out the window and see the ground approaching at alarming speed. We're moving so quickly, I can't get to the carriage window to even try to talk to the Pegasi and help them.

"We're coming in too fast!" Heath yells. "We're going to crash!" Raina closes her eyes tight.

I'm about to do the same when I see Tara pull a sterling silver wand out of a pleat in her dress skirt. It's green and black and has scrollwork I've never seen before. She pulls herself up as the carriage picks up speed. "Suspendanair!" she shouts, and there is a sudden flash. The carriage begins to slow down, but we're still so close to the ground, I don't know if it will help us avoid a crash.

"Brace yourselves!" Sasha shouts as we hold on to loose vines inside the coach. Logan wraps one around his waist.

BOOM! The coach bumps down onto the ground, tossing us around before coming to a stop in the meadow.

I jump out of the carriage to check on the Pegasi. Thankfully they are standing upright and look unhurt, if not a little rattled. I quickly untie them from the carriage.

"Boxer! Ronald! Are you okay?" I neigh. "What happened?"

It's Ronald, Devin. I think he has a bit of food poisoning. It made him ill, and he lost control of the carriage. He nudges the other Pegasus. *I told you that romaine lettuce looked rancid!*

I'm so dizzy! Boxer says. *I need to stay still for a bit. Is everyone all right? I'm so sorry, Devinaria.*

"We're okay," I tell him. "You stay still." Well, at least it wasn't Olivina this time. I feel guilty for checking on the animals first, so I run back to the carriage. "Everyone inside all right?"

Logan and Raina untangle themselves from their vines

and emerge from the carriage along with Tara. Sasha, however, doesn't look good.

She's got a bruise on her forehead, and her eyes look dazed. "I feel dizzy. But I'll be all right. Let's go." She tries to walk and starts to fall. Heath catches her.

"Okay, you're not going anywhere. You stay here with the Pegasi," I say.

"But..." Sasha holds her head. "I..."

"No buts," I tell her.

"Do you think it's a good idea for her to stay here alone?" Logan sounds worried. "She could be captured." He thinks for a moment. "I'll stay with her."

I raise an eyebrow and look at Heath.

"Are you sure?" Heath asks.

"I am," Logan says, sounding surprised himself. "Just don't leave us behind, okay?"

"Never," I promise. "We'll come back for you or send word to Prue to get you out of here."

"The only question is: Who is going to be Princess Scarlet now?" Logan frowns and looks from me to Tara.

"It can't be me," Tara insists. "It just can't."

"I'll do it."

We turn and look at Raina in surprise.

"I know Royal Academy protocol better than any of us," Raina says. "Plus, I schooled Sasha on her fake backstory and everything going on at school. I know Princess Scarlet better than anyone. I can do it."

I love Raina, but she's not the best under pressure. We all know what happened last time she got in front of Olivina.

"Please let me do this," Raina says as if she can hear my thoughts. I don't mention the vine that is currently tangled in her tiara. "I know I can do it, and I want to help." She finds the vine and yanks it out, tilting her tiara.

And somehow I believe her. "I believe you."

"So do I," Heath says with a smile. "Although it feels kind of odd to be your escort."

"Tell me about it." She takes her brother's arm.

We can get them the rest of the way to the front of the castle, Devinaria! Ronald neighs. *We promised we'd get them to the entrance, and we will. We can even do it on land.*

"Thank you," I tell them and look at the others. "They said they can take Heath and Raina."

"But now you only have you and Tara to distract Olivina," Sasha says, her voice weak.

"We will be fine. You just rest," I say with false cheer and smile at Tara. Royal Academy is visible in the distance. It shouldn't be too far of a hike. "I guess we should start walking." I take a step forward and feel my foot slip on something hard. I reach down and pick it up. It's Tara's wand.

"I'll take that," she says. She drops it into the folds of her skirt again. "Might come in handy."

"Yes," I say. "It might."

I don't mention the letter *O* I saw engraved in the silver handle.

THE MASTER OF DISGUISE

Tara's wand has an *O* engraved on it. I only know one person whose name starts with an *O*: Olivina. I have a million questions. Did Tara steal it? Did Olivina give it to her? Is she secretly working with her? My heart beats wildly. Tara seems deathly afraid of the fairy godmother and has been hiding out in the woods to avoid seeing her. None of this makes any sense.

The two of us walk in silence the entire way to the castle. We arrive around the back and pause near the vegetable patch, hiding by the stables. I take a deep breath and give the signal: a birdcall.

A few seconds later, I hear the same birdcall back.

"She's here! Let's go," I tell Tara, hurrying ahead of her and her stolen (borrowed? lended?) wand.

Brynn lifts her lantern into the approaching darkness, and I see her blue eyes light up as we approach. The kitchen at RA is notoriously busy with dozens of chefs cooking to suit every prince's and princess's favorite cuisines. As such, it's the easiest place, according to Logan, to slip in unnoticed. One of several back doors to the kitchen are open, and I can hear pots and pans banging and people shouting requests. Brynn stands in the doorway, her blond hair tucked into a white cap trimmed with a pink ribbon. She's wearing her lady-in-waiting apron and uniform. The two of us run to each other.

"Miss!" Brynn hugs me. "You made it safely!"

I give her an extra-tight squeeze. I hate knowing she's risking her life to help us. The thought of her having to work with Clarissa makes me want to break out in hives. It's so good to see you. Even if this meeting might get us both wanded to the ice caps if we're spotted."

"I've taken every precaution, miss," Brynn says. "I helped Clarissa dress and sent her off to Marta to cover for us with a one-of-a-kind final fitting. All I had to say was 'one-of-a-kind' and 'Marta,' and she was running, miss!"

I laugh. "You'll have to thank Marta for me."

"She misses you. We both do." Brynn's face falls. "Clarissa expects me to trim her hangnails and make sure her night masks don't smudge while she sleeps. I'm so tired, miss, and—oh!" Spotting Tara for the first time, she falters. "Hello."

"Brynn, this is Tara. Tara, meet Brynn," I introduce them. "Tara…" With everything that's been going on, I have no clue how to introduce her, so I just say, "Tara lives at the tree house in the woods you've had Demetris bring letters to. She's been looking out for us while we've been banished."

Brynn beams. "Thank you for taking care of my favorite people."

Tara side-eyes me. "Yes, well, let's get on with the night, shall we?" She slips past us and heads into the hallway. Brynn looks at me worriedly.

"You're not the only one who's had to endure a cranky roommate," I say lightly. I quickly update her on Sasha and Logan and how they're staying behind.

Brynn takes the lead. "I'm afraid you might be too dressed up for the kitchen waitstaff."

"We're not guests too?" Tara asks.

"Sorry for the last-minute change of plans, but every

guest has been accounted for, and you only made aliases for Princess Scarlet and her date," Brynn explains. "I thought there might be a few no-shows whose identities you could take, but this is the event of the season and everyone's showing up. The two of you will be able to get around the castle by posing as ladies-in-waiting who are doubling as waitstaff tonight. Thankfully, I've hidden a few extra uniforms in a sack in the bread pantry. You can change there."

After we change and I make sure Lily and the jewel are safely secured in my new uniform, I'm ready to get to business.

"Kira, any updates?" I ask my kobold.

"Yes!" Kira tells me. "Prue says Olivina's quarters are unoccupied tonight. At the moment, she's greeting the royal court and Princess Scarlet at the entrance to the school." I breathe a sigh of relief that Raina and Heath made it inside.

The scent of baked apples greets me as we near the kitchen again. Brynn pulls us inside where I immediately start coughing.

We are standing in a dust storm of confectioner's sugar.

"Keep sprinkling!" instructs a chef to a group of ladies- and lads-in-waiting standing in front of miniature chocolate ganache cakes. While Logan probably would have opted for the less-is-more approach to cake decorating, this chef has taken a different tactic. "Hazel says Olivina wants each cake covered with sugary perfection! Sugar is Princess Scarlet's favorite ingredient!"

I try not to laugh. This is all for Raina? What exactly did Prue write in her letter to Olivina?

"You three? Why are you just standing there?" A sous chef holding a tray of steamed carrots spots us and frowns. "The appetizer course just went out, and we're prepping the plates for the main course. Shouldn't you be at your stations?"

"Sorry, sir! We're headed over there now." I spot a table where ladies-in-waiting are arranging swirls of potatoes and gravy on plum china plates. (Plum, I believe, is Princess Scarlet's favorite color.) Everyone has their heads down and is busy chopping, prepping, and garnishing. The three of us jump right in.

"Your plate is missing carrots!" the same sous chef yells at me. "Oh!"

I guess the steak on my plate does look kind of lonely without any side dishes.

"Weren't you prepped on the dinner course ahead of time, lady-in-waiting?" the sous chef questions.

I'm not thrilled at his tone. "I have a name. It's..." *Drooping dragons. What is it?*

"*Lila*," Brynn replies. "Why don't you watch me assemble my plate? That way you can get yours out faster than a lion can outrun a dragon."

I grab a pair of tongs to start plating the dish. I get one carrot on the plate when a bell rings. People cover their plates with silver tops and leave the table with them. I follow Brynn and Tara. A chef at the door is watching us head out into the ballroom.

"Heads held high! Smile!" he says. "You are here to serve the royals of this land, and you are thankful for this job Olivina has graciously granted you! Whatever your royal asks of you— whether it be a request for more steak sauce or butter—you grant it! You were placed at RA to serve your royals!"

I bite my lip. This is what ladies- and lads-in-waiting have to hear every day? It's terrible! Why can't we get our own butter or steak sauce?

Brynn gives me a look before entering the room ahead of me. I quickly follow and enter a banquet hall that puts my anniversary ball planning to shame.

Glittering black and green beads and feather-covered

chandeliers match the color scheme and decor on every table in the room. A band I've never heard of (Gnome-More) is playing on the black-and-white-checkered dance floor. They're tiny in stature, but wow, can they play. The royal court watches them from a table on a raised platform near the center of the room, while the Dwarf Police Squad patrols the perimeter. Students have flooded the dance floor in elaborate masks that sparkle and glow. I spot one that flashes the words I RULE.

"What is it about royal gatherings and the need to one-up each other?" I wonder aloud.

"I know," Brynn agrees, her voice in my ear. "I wonder what would happen if we took all the time and energy everyone placed on parties and put it into something really useful like disarming villains or combating ogre breath."

"Who is that girl?" Kira asks in my ear. "I like her."

"Me too," I reply as a couple in full feather headdresses swings by me.

No one seems to notice the parade of ladies- and lads-in-waiting making their way to their tables.

"After we place our dinners, we should be able to slip out of the room unseen," Brynn whispers.

"You three," the chef points to us. "Table sixteen!"

I'm halfway to the table when I realize whose it is: Princess Scarlet's.

Unlike most of the tables that are empty as students dance the night away, theirs is full, and Raina and Heath—Princess Scarlet and her escort—are holding court with Clarissa Hartwith and her roommates.

"Well, finally!" Clarissa says when she sees us. "I thought we'd have to wait all night to get our meals." She turns to Raina. I mean Scarlet! "It's not normally like this here. As Hazel will tell you, we have the best ladies-in-waiting in the kingdom. Normally, those with high royal rankings are served first, but I suspect this one forgot." With an eye roll and a not-so-subtle hand motion toward Brynn, she leans in and whispers. "This is just my temporary lady-in-waiting until Hazel finds me someone more suitable."

I hold my tongue and remind myself why we're here—to oust Olivina and make sure no royal is schooled to think like Clarissa.

"Temporary because three others have already quit on her," one of Clarissa's roommates mumbles to Heath. "Brynn is the only one they could convince to put up with her, and she was only free because of what happened to those other royals a few weeks ago."

"If you ask me, Princess Clarissa, you have poor judgment," Raina speaks up, and I almost drop my platter. "I've heard great things of this Brynn Haun from Hazel, and any princess would be lucky to have her. Maybe she can become mine if I attend RA."

Clarissa's cheeks are a deep shade of plum.

I hear a hoot in my ear and wince. "Way to go, Raina! You tell them!" Kira shouts. "Hey! I can't see!" she cries.

Brynn blushes and stares at the platter she's holding.

"Prue says you guys need to get a move on," Kira tells me. "Olivina is headed to the banquet hall to give her opening remarks."

"I think Princess Scarlet could use some air," says Heath, grabbing Raina's arm and steering her away from the table. "We are going to step outside for a moment. Excuse us."

I suppress a giggle as I set the covered plate in front of Clarissa and follow the others back the way we came. I'm still close enough to hear Clarissa.

"Hey!" she complains. "How come my plate has only one carrot and no sides?"

THE PRINCE IN DISGUISE

We wind up in one of the castle hallways that lead to the dormitory turrets. A group of pixies fly by, but they're moving so fast, I can't pick anyone out. One pixie with a mischievous smile hangs back, bobbing in the air like a hummingbird.

"The ball is over! Go back to your room and go to sleep!" says one with a mischievous smile. Those pixies—what tricksters they are!

I look around, trying to get my bearings. There's a wishing well in an alcove to the right and several mirrors dotting the hallway, along with some of Olivina's aspirational signs. This one has a gleaming glass slipper on it.

> *When the shoe doesn't fit, don't despair!*
> *Maybe it's just time to buy a new pair!*

"Prue can block Milo the Magic Mirror from seeing you in the halls, but you need to get to Olivina's private quarters ASAP."

Heath is holding his ear and listening to the same message I just received. "How do we remember which hallway leads to Olivina?"

"It's easy! It's to the right." Raina spins around and frowns. "Or maybe it's to the left."

The three of us fan out. Tara isn't helping at all.

"Any clue where it could be?" I ask, thinking again of her wand.

She blinks rapidly and won't look at me. "No. I've only been up there once."

I'm no mind reader, but I'm pretty sure she's lying. What if this is another one of her traps like that day she found us in the forest? What if she's already tipped off Olivina that we're here? What if the two of them have been planning this moment all along? "Maybe your wand knows the way," I say lightly.

"My wand?" Tara repeats, blinking again. "I don't think so. I don't know a spell for finding hidden rooms."

"Are you sure?" I press. "Because I think you do know."

"Devin? What's going on?" Heath asks.

"Prue says stop fighting and find it!" Kira tells me.

But I can't hold back my feelings any longer. "I want to know why the wand Tara is carrying has an *O* on it. Aren't wands engraved with their owner's names? Tara's has an *O*, which, if you ask me, stands for Olivina." Raina audibly inhales.

"It doesn't," Tara insists, but she's looking at her feet.

I won't let her hurt my friends. "I don't believe you. I think you're leading us into another trap!"

"Everyone calm down," Heath locks eyes with me. "Tara, can you explain where you got that wand, please?"

"What does it matter?" Tara throws her hands up. "It's not like anything we do here is going to change Enchantasia!"

"Change happens when people take action!" I say.

"Olivina is the one who makes all the decisions, and she's not going to give that power up!" Tara argues.

"We can't sit here and do nothing!" I insist. "We need to be the change this kingdom needs." Brynn is standing behind Tara and gives me a silent fist bump to the air.

She exhales, the anger from a moment ago gone. "Sometimes you can't make people change, no matter how much you want them to. This is a fool's errand." She throws down her cap. Brynn swoops in and picks it up. "And I don't want to be part of it." She starts walking away.

"What is going on here?" Kira shrieks.

"Fine! Run away. You're good at that!" I look at the others. They look uncomfortable. "What? She's been so standoffish and afraid to face Olivina for so long. Well, you know what? I'm afraid too, but I'm here, trying to make a difference. Trying to get my life back and save everyone else unknowingly caught under her spell. I can't just sit by in silence!" I suddenly become aware of the fact that the others are all staring at me. "Her wand is really Olivina's. I'm sure of it!"

"Why would she have her wand?" Heath says.

"I don't know, but she does." I stare at her retreating figure. "If she wants to live her life alone, then let her. She's not helping us anyway."

"The important thing right now is to find Olivina's office." Raina walks around looking at every detail of the architecture. "Aha! Now I remember. We need to find the glass slipper!"

"The glass slipper?" Heath repeats.

"Yes! It's one of her most famous wishes, so she keeps a reminder of it in the castle to help her get where she most wants to go—and at RA, it's her own office." Raina peers under a table. "Now where would one be in the hallway? I'm sure it's not just out in the open, or princesses would be trying it on all day long."

"Perhaps I can help."

Professor Pierce is standing right behind us. He looks exactly as I remembered. We, however, look nothing like our real selves.

"You've been spotted! Abort!" Kira yells, tugging on my earlobe.

"Good evening, Professor," I say and curtsy like a good princess, or, in my case, lady-in-waiting, would, hoping he thinks we're visiting students. The others bow or curtsy as well.

Professor Pierce smiles. "I was wondering when you'd all turn up. I didn't expect it to be so soon. Well done."

I feel panicked. "Pardon?"

"Sometimes those who hide in the shadows offer the brightest lights," he says coyly. "Hello, young Devin."

I freeze. "I…"

Raina grabs my arm. "Actually, this is my potential lady-in-waiting. You see, I'm Princess Scarlet from a nearby kingdom, and I'm considering coming to this school."

He holds out his hand to shake her free one. "It's good to see you too, Raina and Heath. Brynn, I suggest you head back to the banquet before Clarissa gets too wound up about not being able to find you and alerts Hazel."

Brynn's eyes widen. "Good idea." She gives me a hug. "Stay safe, miss!"

"You too," I tell her and look back at the professor. "How did you…?"

His eyes sparkle. "A good prince can always see through to the truth."

"Red said something about that," Raina says. "Why would you hide being royal?"

He blushes slightly. "I don't talk about it much. It's part of my agreement with the fairy godmother. I was once under Olivina's tutelage just like you were. I, too, was told I had a promising future in this kingdom as a prince who would sit on the royal court. But when my vision for Enchantasia didn't match the fairy godmother's, I found myself on the outs. I tried to change the way things worked at this school, but one voice wasn't strong enough to tip the balance."

I feel sad for Professor Pierce. How lonely it would have been to go on this journey alone.

"She didn't banish you?" Heath asks.

Professor Pierce pursues his lips. "I discovered some information that Olivina didn't want made public. In exchange for my silence, I was allowed to stay here, under her watch, and teach. I've made peace with my decision, but I've always been disappointed in myself for not speaking up when I had the chance." He looks at me. "But when I met you and your friends, I thought, 'Maybe these are the children who could do what I couldn't.' Which is why I put you in touch with our friends in the woods. How are they?"

"Good. I think they miss home, but Tara likes it in the woods," I add.

The professor looks puzzled. "Tara? Ah, yes, I remember Red Riding Hood mentioning her, though I've never had the opportunity to meet her myself."

Heath and I look at each other. "You don't know Tara personally? I thought you would have had her as a student,"

I say. "I think she was taught privately. She was supposedly Olivina's favorite."

Professor Pierce frowns. "I usually know all our students. I do remember a Corden and Prue, who were both banished last year."

"We met them," Heath explains. "They're the whole reason we got this far today."

The professor ponders for a moment. "I remember Prue being very talented at working the castle's mirrors and Corden had exceptional taste, but I don't remember Tara."

More warning bells go off in my head. How could one of the most popular professors at this school not know Tara?

"But if it's Olivina you seek, I fear you may have missed your chance," the professor says. "She is already on the way to the ball." He raises his right eyebrow. "Unless you're hoping to visit her quarters when she is not there."

"Professor Pierce?" A mirror down the hall lights up, and everyone jumps. It's Milo the Magic Mirror, who is Olivina's spy. "Is that you I hear? There is an issue with my connection this evening, and I can't get you in view. Olivina is concerned there is a problem and would like to confer with you at once."

Professor Pierce holds a finger to his lips. "Of course,

Milo! I'll be right there." He looks at Raina. "You always knew your Royal Academy rules better than anyone." Raina blushes. "And you're correct—you need to find a glass slipper to enter Olivina's quarters." He gives her a look. "So I must ask you: Where is a princess most likely to leave a slipper behind, knowing it will be found?"

Raina lights up. "On the main staircase, of course, where it will be seen!"

He bows slightly to her. "You are correct. I look forward to you returning to class soon. All of you. Good luck." With that, he slips down the hall and out of sight.

"Here!" Raina says, pointing to the main stairs that lead to the classrooms on the second floor. She searches around wildly for a slipper. I don't see one, and neither does she. "It has to be here," she says to herself. "Then again, Olivina wouldn't want us all finding it, or students would be stopping by daily, which is why…" She spins around and squeals, pointing to a statue on the staircase. "She'd place it in a pumpkin!" She rushes over to the statue, lifts the lid to the ceramic pumpkin, and pulls out a tiny glass slipper. She presses her thumb to the heel, and a doorway behind us appears. A large gold *O* is engraved on the shimmering silver door. It's the entrance to Olivina's quarters!

"Raina, I don't tell you this enough, but you're brilliant," Heath says.

She shrugs and steps through the doorway. "I know. Now hurry. We don't know how long that doorway will stay open."

"There's something I still don't get," I say as we rush toward the door. "Sasha and I found letters to Tara in our dorm room when we were students, so we assumed she was also a student at some point. Snow knows her, so she had to be. But Professor Pierce tutors everyone. Why wouldn't he remember her?" I duck as a pixie flies dangerously close to my head. I can't stop thinking there is part of the puzzle I'm missing. Why was Tara so afraid to face Olivina? And where did she just run off to? "Do you think Logan and Sasha are okay?" I ask.

"They're fine," Heath says, stepping through the doorway. "They're together. We have to do what we came here to do."

I know Heath's right, but I can't get rid of this feeling something is wrong. "Tara is friends with Prue. Are we sure we can trust her?"

"Hey!" Kira tugs on my ear. "I love Prue."

I forgot she was even in there. "I just mean…" I hold my chest. My heart is beating fast. I can't put my finger on what feels wrong.

Heath extends his hand back through the shimmering door, which seems to be fading. "This is our one shot to take Olivina down. Let's finish this, and then we'll learn the real story. Okay?"

I hesitate, staring at his outstretched hand for a second, then grab it. He pulls me through the door as it starts to crackle and disappear. For a moment, I feel icy cold and see nothing but darkness, but then the world comes into focus, just like a mirror making a connection. We're in Olivina's rose-scented office, which is filled with pink and purple furnishings and lots of gold accents. A wall of mirrors is projecting a live feed of every inch of the castle, but I don't see Tara on any of them.

"Prue says Olivina is almost done with her speech," Kira tells me. "She wants to know where Tara is, and why this is taking so long. She said, 'Maybe she should have just been here herself because when you want something done right you—'"

"Shh!" I scold Kira. "I'm thinking. Which mirror is the one we're supposed to hack?"

Raina keeps her eye on the door. "Being in here feels creepy. Pick a mirror, and be fast!"

My eyes trail from one mirror to the next—looking at the ballroom, the rose garden, Marta working in the Royal Underground, even the Enchanted Garden where I see workers bewitching pumpkins into coaches. Finally, my eyes land on one mirror that is a reflection of the room. It's the only mirror that appears to be an actual mirror.

"There!" I yell and go straight for it. I pull the tiny pink jewel out of my pocket and hold it up. Prue did an impeccable job of making it look exactly like the other jewels on this frame. Olivina will never know it's there. "Pry one out so we can stick in this jewel and get out of here," I tell Heath, my palms beginning to sweat. I'm getting nervous too. Lily flicks her tongue over and over again, saying, *Hurry! Hurry!*

"Already on it." Heath wedges a small letter opener between the jewel and the frame. I can see the sweat on his brow.

"Quickly!" Kira tells me. "We don't have much time. She could be back any minute."

"I know," I hiss, watching Heath work. My heart is still beating wildly. "Raina, you stand—"

Lookout was the word I would have said, but I don't get a chance. A gust of wind blows through the room, sending

Raina, Heath, and me flying backward, the all-important jewel tumbling out of my hands. I hit my head on Olivina's desk when I tumble and instinctively grab it, wincing at the pain. I can't focus enough to get up.

Olivina has her wand aimed at my heart. "Hello there, Devinaria. I think you already know each other."

My head is throbbing, but I manage to lift it to see who she's talking about.

It's Tara, and she's standing beside Olivina as if it's exactly where she belongs.

THE FINAL COUNTDOWN

I hear a sob escape Raina's throat. Her right foot is caught under a fallen armoire. I can see the panic in her eyes as we make eye contact. *Where's Heath?* I freak out. I spot him on the floor under a broken window. He's not moving. My hands are shaking, but I tap my ear, trying to get Kira's attention without alerting the fairy godmother to her. She's silent. Was she thrown from my ear? I feel my dress pocket and realize it is also empty. *Where is Lily?* Frantically, I feel the floor around me even though it hurts to move. Lily is nowhere to be seen.

"Now, now, Devin, don't be frightened." Olivina's voice is soothing as she walks over the broken glass and fallen mirrors to stand directly over me. "Yes, I know it's you and your friends even though your appearances are masked. Such a clever boy, that Corden." She glances at Raina who is struggling. "Such a smart move disguising yourself as a new student. I didn't think you had it in you, Raina! Princess Scarlet would have been the perfect addition to RA. Alas, I knew it couldn't be true. She was just too perfect, wasn't she?"

Olivina inches closer, and I struggle to move away. Even though she's under five feet tall, she seems like a giant thanks to her glass heels and her hair stacked high on her head. One of her heels steps on my skirt, pinning me to the floor. She shifts her weight onto that foot and looks at me over the folds of her satin skirt. "Take a deep breath, child. Your friends are fine."

They don't look fine. My head is pounding, Heath is unconscious, Raina is pinned to the floor, Lily and Kira are missing. And Logan and Sasha...

"Oh! There's no need to worry about your *other* friends either." It's as if Olivina heard my thoughts, because with a wave of her wand, Logan and Sasha appear in a corner of the room. They've been bound and are sitting back-to-back. They look around in surprise, see me, and start talking at the same time.

"Devin! The gargoyles! They're here!" Logan scrunches

up his nose. "Their breath is worse than an ogre's, if you can believe it!"

Sasha glares at Olivina as she holds her head. "I knew you were behind this!"

"Behind what?" Olivina asks. "I knew you wouldn't come on your own so I brought you here. You were already trespassing on school grounds despite your banishment." She looks back at me, and her smile is sinister. "I'm not going to hurt you, Devin. I'm not going to hurt any of you. I just want to talk. I hate how we left things last time."

"Tara!" Sasha cries. "Don't just stand there. Do something! Help us!"

Olivina laughs so hard she has to hold her stomach. "Yes, Tara, who do you want to help, dear?"

As she steps off my skirt and moves toward her desk, I scoot backward, finally free from her glass heel. Where are Lily and Kira—not to mention the jewel? As I scan the room, I think I see something move by Heath's shirt, but I can't be sure.

"Do you want to finally tell these people—your new friends from the forest—who you really are?" Olivina asks.

Tara's eyes blink rapidly as she looks from Olivina to us and back again. She is holding a chair next to her for dear life.

"Tara?" Raina questions. "Remember what we said: we'll never leave you."

Olivina laughs. "Such lies! They already left you once tonight—when they let you run off into the castle. Devin doesn't think much of you, as you know. Do you really think she'll have your back? Or will she leave you behind again?"

"The headmistress is right about one thing," I try, stalling for time so I can find the jewel. "I'm not a fan of Tara's. She's a liar." Tara winces. I slide to the left and glance at the broken vase and flowers lying in water on the floor. No jewel. "Just be honest with us, for the first time since we met. You never went to Royal Academy, did you?"

"Oh my gnomes, you can't be serious!" Sasha moans.

"I saw her wand," I tell the others. "It has Olivina's mark on it."

"But..." Sasha says. "Snow knew her! And the notes..."

I cut her off before she says too much. "She lied to all of us about who she really is." Olivina looks tickled pink watching us work this out.

"But she saved us in the woods." Logan looks confused. "Didn't she?"

Tara looks away again, but I notice her hands gripping the chair so hard they're turning purple.

"Don't be fooled," I tell them. "Tara showed up to make us disappear, not help us. But then we were caught by that firebird, and the others felt bad for us so she had to bring us back to the tree house. She never really wanted to help us. Did you, Tara?"

"Yes, tell them, Tara," Olivina adds, waving her wand gaily. "Tell them why you didn't want them knowing who you really are. Why you tried to dissuade Corden and Prue from hiding out with you in the first place? Why you went off the grid and stayed away for so long? I'll admit, I didn't think you had the gumption to live in the woods like that for so long, but you did. You've impressed me, child. And now you're back. You might as well tell them why."

I notice something moving near Raina's skirt and blink twice to be sure. I think it's Lily!

"Tara?" Logan tries. "What is she talking about?"

"Olivina knows who I really am." Tara chokes as if the words hurt her. "It's not safe to be near me. I tried to get you guys to go away, but you kept acting like you could actually change how things work. Don't you know by now you can't?"

Her eyes are pained. "There is no winning with the fairy godmother."

Olivina looks at her fingernails. "Don't be so formal, Tara. Call me Grandmother." Raina inhales sharply.

"Grandmother?" I repeat.

"Yes, imagine living up to that legacy, Devin!" Olivina says brightly. "To be the only living relative of the greatest fairy godmother there ever was. To know you'd have to take over for her someday...and yet not want to."

"Because what you're doing here is evil!" Tara cries, hot tears falling down her face. "I don't want any part of what you're planning for Enchantasia!"

Alarm bells go off in my head. "What does she mean?"

"I raised her," Olivina says. "I taught her everything I know, and when I realized the strength of her magic, I tried to cultivate her power."

"You tried to make me my mother, and I'm not!" Tara shouts.

"Oh, Tara, always so short-sighted." Olivina shakes her head. "Your mother wasn't strong enough to control her own magic. That was her downfall. It had nothing to do with me. But you, from the time you were a baby, I could see you were different. You were so curious. So open to learning. I knew you could be great in a way your mother never could be. So I tried to give you power you could never attain because you're not royal." She looks at me. "Tara could not openly go here because she's not of royal descent, but that doesn't mean I wouldn't bend the rules when it came to my own flesh and blood. I had her taught by Snow in private. I kept her here as a lady-in-waiting, also teaching her myself at night and in private."

"So that's why you once lived in our dorm room," Sasha realizes. "You were a lady-in-waiting for other students." Tara is crying harder now.

I glance at Raina's skirt again. I haven't imagined it. It really is moving. A small orange snout pops out. Lily! This time, Raina spots her too. Lily slips out from under the skirt, and I notice something on her back. It's Kira! In her small hand, I see she has the missing jewel. Raina and I lock eyes. Olivina and Tara need to be distracted until that jewel can be placed in the mirror.

"You could have been more powerful than I ever could be," Olivina says to Tara. "The plans I had for you. For me. For the two of us."

"I won't do your evil work." Tears run down Tara's cheeks.

"I tried to stay away so she couldn't find me. So I couldn't hurt anyone." Tara looks at me. "But you were so convincing. I thought maybe…"

Tara wasn't evil. She was just alone in her decisions and misunderstood. Just like I was when I was forced to come to Royal Academy. My stomach twists as I think about how harsh I've been. But I can make it up to her. I'm not alone now, and either is she.

"You thought she could defeat me," Olivina finishes. "Foolish girl. Who could defeat me when I have the royal court on my side?"

Lily and Kira begin inching along the debris, passing Heath, who is just starting to stir.

"Devin?" Olivina asks. "Have you nothing to say about all this? You know I find it rude when princesses are speechless. I'm trying to have a conversation with you! I'm awfully sorry about how things have gone down, dear. I never wanted to banish any of you. You were such promising prospects. With your gift of talking to animals, I knew you could be a tremendous asset to Tara and me when the time came."

Heath sits up as Lily and Kira near the mirror. I double down on keeping Olivina distracted.

"But we didn't follow your rules so we had to go, is that right?" I stall.

"Yes," Olivina says solemnly. "It's unfortunate. Everyone is upset by it—poor Snow, and all of your parents, of course. I hate creating spectacles like this! It makes people ask questions, and as you might have guessed, I don't like questions." Her nostrils flare. "But you just wouldn't leave well enough alone."

I quickly glance at Heath. He's shifted toward the wall so Lily can climb onto his leg. *Almost there.*

"You wanted us to be mini versions of you," I say. "You don't want royals who think for themselves. You want royals who only listen to you."

Olivina laughs. "Exactly! I wouldn't have spent so many years courting royals if I didn't desperately want to be one myself. I think your father realized that. It's a pity. I like your father, but…at least with Prue and Corden, their families are so uninvolved that there were ways to make them go away. But your lot seems more persistent. If you refuse to fall in line, I might have to arrange an accident."

Heath plucks the jewel from Kira's hand and slowly reaches toward the mirror.

"I don't want you to be angry, Devin," Olivina says. "When I lost Tara, I thought, who could join me? Who could I cultivate like Snow, Ella, Rapunzel, and Rose and make them think and act just as I do? Of course, the students here all are taught to do that, but they're not really strong enough to lead the way I want Enchantasia led."

Heath slips the jewel into the hole on the mirror.

"Are you listening, Devin?" Olivina snaps. "I'm trying to tell you why I've worked so hard to keep this school running exactly the way I want it to run—at least until my grand-daughter could take over!" Her voice thunders, making the room shake. A vase falls off a shelf and crashes to the floor. "You could at least listen to me!"

Something inside me snaps. Last time I was in this room—actually every time I was in this room—I let Olivina make all the decisions. I let Sasha put together the pieces. I was a passive participant. (At least, I think that's what Professor Shoeburn, my professor for The Royal Within seminar, called it.) But I don't want to be a passive participant anymore. Being quiet doesn't help change things. Making your voice heard does. Professor Pierce taught me that just tonight.

"I am listening, but this time around I have something to say too," I reply.

Olivina looks mildly amused. "Do you now, young princess?"

"I do! You're a bully, a liar, and a lousy fairy godmother. I won't let you control me anymore."

"Ooh! Listen to that fire in your belly!" Olivina says with a laugh. "I suspect with proper training, you could have been the greatest princess I ever mentored."

If there's any chance Prue was able to hijack the feed, I need to keep Olivina talking. "Why do you think that? Is it because you trained the royal court to do exactly what you want them to do?"

"Of course! Don't you see? I did all of this to help Enchantasia," Olivina tells the room. "I did it to protect us. And to get the power I couldn't attain on my own, of course. If I hadn't helped Ella get her glass slipper, she'd still be a commoner! If I hadn't found the prince to wake up Snow, she'd still be asleep! Just like Rose! And Rapunzel in that tower... How do you think she was found?"

"But you didn't just help them," I say calmly. "First you twisted their tales by putting them in harm's way so you could be the one who figured out how they could be rescued! And you did it all so they'd think they couldn't manage ruling without you. Isn't that right?

"Do you think a lowly lady-in-waiting like myself could have risen to power if I didn't have the right connections? No!" She glares at me. "It's all about the royals in Enchantasia, and once I knew I could never become one or marry one, I set my sights on the princesses who could help me climb the ladder of power. They can't make a move without me now. And as the next generations of royals ascend, I make sure they, too, lead the way *I* want them to lead. To make the agreements *I* want them to make. To make sure they fear the things *I* want them to fear so that they never lose sight of how much they need me. And, when the day comes, they will need Tara." She looks at her granddaughter. "She can never escape her destiny and survive in this kingdom. I'm helping her!"

Olivina looks at all of us. "Want to come back from banishment?" She looks at Raina pointedly. "Then promise you'll fall in line. If you do, I can make all of your troubles disappear just like that." She snaps her fingers, and Logan and Sasha's bindings unwind. The armoire lifts off Raina. "You just have to trust me."

But I don't want to be someone's prisoner. If the royal court really knew they were puppets on a string like Pinocchio, they wouldn't want to be either.

"Never," I say.

"Never," Raina agrees. One by one, my friends all say the same thing. It's only Tara who is still quiet.

Olivina's smile fades. "What a pity. Tara? Finish them."

"What?" Tara pushes herself against the wall. Olivina makes her command clear.

"Use your wand, and make them disappear. For good."

"Tara! Don't listen to her!" Raina cries.

"Do it!" Olivina shouts as tears stream down Tara's face.

"Tara, listen to me," I say softly. "You don't have to do this. I'm sorry I didn't understand what you were going through. I'm sorry I didn't ask you what was really going on, but Olivina is wrong. You're not alone anymore. You have us. You can fight her!" Tara looks away and back again. "I believe in you!"

"I don't have a choice," Tara sobs. "I'm sorry."

"Don't do this!" Sasha begs.

"Finish them!" Olivina thunders.

Tara shakily points the wand at me, and Raina screams.

Heath lunges for Tara, but in his weakened state, he's too slow. I close my eyes and wait to disappear. But then, I hear something fall to the floor, and I open my eyes. Tara has thrown her wand.

"I can't do it," she tells her grandmother. "I won't."

"You listen to me, dearie," Olivina says, advancing on her.

Boom! The doors to the room open, and Snow and Professor Pierce burst through them.

"Stop!" Snow thunders.

"Snow!" Olivina looks frazzled. "What are you doing here?"

"We know, Olivina," Snow says sadly. "We've seen it all. Everyone has."

"Olivina!" Hazel cries, running in behind them. "Stop talking! Your quarters are being projected on all of the mirrors in the banquet hall!"

"Everyone is watching," Professor Pierce says. "The truth has finally been revealed."

Olivina looks from the mirrors to Tara to me, and then she starts to shake. Her hands crunch up in desperation and she lets out an ear-piercing scream. It shatters the glass in the mirrors and makes the walls around us start to crumble. My friends and I dive for cover, but there's nowhere safe to go.

"Look out!" Snow cries, as Professor Pierce pulls her out of harm's way and into another room.

But it's too late for us. We cling to each other and brace for impact, but nothing happens. I look up and realize Tara is standing over us, her wand creating a protective shell over our frames.

"Foolish, foolish children!" Olivina shouts. "You have no idea what you have done! All of Enchantasia will regret this." She locks eyes with me. "You haven't heard the last from me!" And with a wave of her wand, she's gone.

BREAKING NEWS: Royal Academy

Headmistress Revealed to Be a Villain!

Flees School and Cannot Be Found

By Timmy Targowski

Earlier this evening, Headmistress Olivina, our kingdom's beloved and esteemed fairy godmother, was caught on magic mirror making some questionable statements about the nature of her relationship with the royal court. According to eyewitnesses at the royal-only ball, a view of Olivina's private quarters was projected into the banquet hall by magic mirror. Students and the Dwarf Police Squad heard her confess to being the orchestrator of several fairy-tale catastrophes—and happy endings—in this kingdom.

"If what we heard is correct, Olivina didn't actually *save* our princesses from peril," says Dwarf Police Chief Pete. "She put them in peril in the first place so that she could be the one to rescue them. All to make sure her guidance was the one they sought more than any other."

By the time law enforcement realized what was happening, Princess Snow and Professor Pierce of Royal Academy had already reached Olivina in her chambers, where she was arguing with several students whose identities have not yet been revealed. "When she was backed into a corner, she used magic to disappear," Pete reveals. "That's a shame because our men are the best in the biz and we could have nabbed her. If, you know, we were there."

HEAS has been flooded with reports of sightings of Olivina this evening, but the fairy godmother has yet to be found. A widespread search is currently underway for both her and a rumored granddaughter who the fairy godmother kept hidden from the royal court. "That girl saved the other students' lives and went against Olivina to protect them. She's a hero!" (More on this estranged granddaughter of Olivina as soon as we have it!)

Allegations as dark as these are sure to cause panic alongside rumors of Rumpelstiltskin and the wicked fairy Alva preparing an attack on Enchantasia. Could Olivina be in cahoots with them? Princess Snow says all will be revealed in its own time.

"Tonight, a veil has been lifted," Snow said to the press following the incident. "The royal court and I vow to get to the bottom of what has happened with Olivina, and to ensure that *all* students, even the ones banished by Olivina, have a chance at a bright future in Enchantasia. We vow to make Royal Academy the place Olivina always promised it to be—the true training ground for the fairy-tale leaders of tomorrow."

◇◇◇◇◇◇◇

COMING IN TWO WEEKS, A NEW COLUMN from the creator of the *Enchantasia Insider*, Sasha Briarwood! "Royal Academy: The Revolution" will follow the changes at the kingdom's school for royals and what we can hope to see from their students in the future. Don't miss it: only in *Happily Ever After Scrolls*.

ACKNOWLEDGMENTS

Kate Prosswimmer, you are my fellow outlaw and partner in crime! I could not ask for a better person to be on this Royal Academy journey with. I love our process, and I love our brainstorming sessions! I am a lucky author indeed.

To the team at Sourcebooks, including Dominque Raccah, Todd Stocke, Steve Geck, Margaret Coffee, Heidi Weiland, Valerie Pierce, Sean Murray, Chris Bauerle, Beth Oleniczak, Heather Moore, Mallory Hyde, Stefani Sloma, Lizzie Lewandowski, Nicole Hower, and Cassie Gutman. I am so blessed to work with such amazing people. Thank you for all you do to spread the word about Royal Academy!

And to Mike Heath—I get so many questions about your incredible images for these fairy-tale books. Thank you for continuing to surprise me with the most incredible covers!

To Dan Mandel, my agent, without whom I'd be lost on this journey. Thank you for always helping me steer the ship in the right direction. I'm so lucky to be working with you.

I'm so thankful for this middle-grade and YA community that I hold so dearly, and have endless thanks for Elizabeth Eulberg, Kieran Scott (once more, with feeling!), Courtney Sheinmel, Katie Sise, Sarah Mlynowski, Julia Devillers, Lindsay Currie, Tiffany Schmidt, and extraordinary library friends Rose Brock, Kelly Rechsteiner, and Vanessa Schroeder.

To all friends and family who help me do what I do every day and make the juggling look easy (even when it's not): Christi Lennon, Joanie Cook, Elpida Argenziano, Kristen Marino, Lisa Gagliano, AnnMarie Pullicino, Marcy Miller, my sister Nicole and my parents (for always stepping in and helping with the kids when I'm on tour—and for stopping in every library they see on road trips to see whether they carry my books!).

I can't imagine living in Cinderella's castle (a girl can dream!) without my boys: Mike, for the endless love, advice, and support; Tyler, for reading my work and always trying to make it more "exciting"; Dylan, the best cheerleader a mom could ask for; and my chihuahua writing partners, Jack Sparrow and Ben Kenobi.

Finally, to my readers: Nothing makes me happier than hearing from you! Whether it's a note, an email, or a conversation we've had at a signing, I feel so blessed to meet you and share this fairy-tale adventure with you. I hope you're enjoying your time in Enchantasia as much as I am.

ABOUT THE AUTHOR

Jen Calonita has inter-
viewed everyone from Reese
Witherspoon to Justin
Timberlake, but the only
person she's ever wanted to
trade places with is Disney's
Cinderella. When Jen isn't
plotting, she's working on stories in the Fairy Tale Reform
School series and in her new

Royal Academy Rebels series. She lives in Merrick, New York, with her husband, two sons, and their Chihuahuas. Visit Jen at jencalonitaonline.com.

Don't Miss

FAIRY TALE REFORM SCHOOL

An Enchantasia series from Jen Calonita

Our mission: To turn wicked delinquents and former villains into future heroes.